The Rules of the Game.

"The deal is this," Cal said. "I get you into Omega Space. You get me back home."

"Deal, Calspar Shemzak?" said the Jaxdron.

"Let's put it this way. Rules. To a game. And that's the game. I help you win, and the rule is: you take me home."

The rippling of amusement again. "Oh, no, Calspar Shemzak. The rule is: you cooperate, or you experience pain and affliction unlike anything you've ever imagined."

"Gee," said Cal. "And you were starting to act like such nice guys."

Ace Science Fiction Books by David Bischoff

TIN WOODMAN
(with Dennis R. Bailey)

The Star Hounds Series
THE INFINITE BATTLE
GALACTIC WARRIORS
THE MACROCOSMIC CONFLICT

STARHOUNDS

BOOK THREE

THE MACROCOSMIC CONFLICT

DAVID BISCHOFF

ACE SCIENCE FICTION BOOKS
NEW YORK

This book is an Ace Science Fiction
original edition, and has never been
previously published.

THE MACROCOSMIC CONFLICT

An Ace Science Fiction Book / published by arrangement with
the author

PRINTING HISTORY
Ace Science Fiction edition / February 1986

ISBN: 0-441-78169-1

Ace Science Fiction Books are published by
The Berkley Publishing Group,
200 Madison Avenue, New York, New York 10016.
PRINTED IN THE UNITED STATES OF AMERICA

For Ted White

Chapter One

He hung crucified on the galaxy.

His arms were bound to the spiral arms by rings of buzzing force. His legs dangled, wrapped in starglow.

The stars burned his back. The echoes of other galaxies distantly hissed. Martyr, they whispered. A martyr for physics!

"I die," said Calspar Shemzak, "for my race. I die for humanity!"

"Come now, Mr. Shemzak," came the Jaxdron voice. "We know you have a tendency for the melodramatic, but don't you think that this is a bit ridiculous?"

Cal Shemzak opened his eyes.

The stars dissolved into dark spots in his vision. These faded as well, into the cool light of the conference room.

He sat in a chair.

He was still clad in his khaki-colored jumpsuit, though now he also wore a helmet. To this helmet was attached wires that snaked up to myriad color-coded connections on the wall behind him. Force-bands bound arms and legs to the chair.

"The more you cooperate, the easier it will be," continued the Jaxdron voice. "You have been a playful and clever gamesman thus far. Please do not think that we do not appreciate your efforts, your spirit. However, now we need your cooperation, Calspar Shemzak. We need your most marvelous mind to work with the other minds that we have created."

Cal Shemzak's eyes focused upon the Jaxdron relaxing in the gravity baths across from him. What ugly bastards they were! Cal thought, though he usually didn't make physical judgments about aliens, preferring a more scientific view. He supposed his evaluation was based more on his hatred of these particular aliens—earned hatred—than anything else.

Less than two meters tall, they were humanoid in form, with very large jade eyes, large lippy mouths, and noses that would not look too out of place on tiny Terran elephants. Translator speaker boxes hung nearby: attachments for the interrogation. Wreaths of gas and mist bathed their light-red skin, channeled by gravity modulators below. Occasionally one of the beings would dip its mouth into dense packs of brown and cerulean mists, suck deeply, then casually exhale the stuff—gray now—through uplifted proboscis. Air intake ducts caught these cloud streams and drew them away. The creatures looked like nothing more than a bunch of human genetic freaks at a ricti smoking bash.

"I don't have much control over my unconscious visualizations," Cal answered in his own good time. "You should know that by now. You've been picking my brain long enough!"

"Yes, with great enjoyment." The central creature was the principal spokesman. This was the first Jaxdron that Cal had actually encountered, several hours before, in the room full of his clones. "You have quite an active imagination, human. The interweavings of symbols and play added a great deal of spice to our analysis and provided additional depth to several strata of gaming."

"I hope you realize that this is no game for me!" Cal shot back angrily.

"Only because you are not sufficiently enlightened, human." The sentence was oddly stressed in places—a clear tip-off to its translated nature. Otherwise, the voice was disconcertingly like Cal's own in timbre and tone. "Perhaps at the end of this session you will be better educated, and appreciate the joys open to you in your role with us."

"Role? Wonderful. You mean you're going to tell me why you grabbed me from Mulliphen, destroyed our project, spirited me to one planet, gave me a butler—of all goddamned things—and then shuttled me to another planet? Why you've been putting me through paces like a rat in a lab? Why you've created dozens of creatures that look just like me? If knowing my role has anything to do with the answers to those questions, I welcome that knowledge a lot!"

The flesh of the creatures turned a deeper red and quivered. A sign of some sort of emotion? The response from the speaker seemed to indicate that. "Oh, yes, you are playing! We do so much enjoy learning the various means of language play employed by different races. The more advanced, the more complex!"

"What do you mean? I'm the sort who plays along—I mean, who goes with the flow. You know that by now, surely. But as to playing with you—"

"Come, come, now, Cal Shemzak," the Jaxdron admonished. "You know why we have taken the trouble to capture you of all other Terrans. You are a physicist of quite amazing mental powers. We wish to unlock that dimension you call Omega Space and so extend the sphere of our jovial cavortings farther, so that we may have better games with the Infinity of Existence."

"Omega Space, huh? But listen, guys, that's what the project on Mulliphen, by the Interspacial Fault, was all about! And we weren't very close to cracking the problem at all. I was about the only one who really had a chance."

"Precisely. Which is why we wanted you. So simple. Despite the subtleties and complexities of Play, in essence, everything is very simple. Wisdom for you, Terran. Do accept our gift. And please do join in with our Joyous Celebrations!"

"You mean, cooperate. Direct my thoughts in the ways you wish."

"Exactly. You claim to be a reed that bends, and yet

now all your many symbols are conflicting with our wishes."

"No game this time, huh?"

"Games must have rules, Calspar Shemzak!"

"So tell me what this has to do with all my copies out there!" Cal tried to twist his head toward the other room, but could not: the helmet would not permit the movement.

In buzzing, clicking voices, the Jaxdron seemed to confer amongst each other for a time. Then the central alien spoke: "Yes, there is no more reason for hiding matters, Terran. You have provided much amusement in our study of you, but now is the time for clear speaking. As stated before, we Jaxdron wish to find the secrets of Omega Space. We wish to penetrate that dimension. You have the key to unlock our desire. But not by yourself. I presume, Cal Shemzak, you are aware of the basic workings of the organ in your body known as the brain."

Cal found that he was able to shrug. "Sure. Synapses and neurons, matrices . . . stuff like that."

"Yes, well . . . good enough. In simple language, not only is your particular human mind wired in such a way as to be very skilled in the talents of a top physicist, but the psychic energies produced by your problem-solving in that area harmonize and link to cosmic energies. This is called many things by your race. Intuition. ESP. This is your special gift; and you have trained yourself well in its use. It is unique. Certainly none of our race owns such a talent, which is why we bother with you.

"However, quite simply, it is not good enough."

"Huh?" Cal blinked, then grinned broadly. "Well, then you can let me go, can't you? Could you just ship me back to Earth? That would be very nice!"

"Ah, your playful spirit again, Cal Shemzak." Again, the rippling of its mottled flesh: mirth. "It is refreshing to see it returning in such full force. Now please let us continue."

"Just trying."

"Understandable. We had hoped that by merely putting your brain through prescribed paces, our process would work in you subconsciously. But apparently this is not true, as your rebellious nature, as illustrated in this past session, proves. Perhaps if we detailed to your rational thinking process our desires, and engaged your willing cooperation, your subsconscious will also cooperate."

"Well, maybe, yeah. So get on with it. I'm all tied up with suspense!"

In their gravity baths the aliens looked like contorted planets, swathed in clouds, orbiting some unseen sun.

"We determined your essential singular inadequacy while studying you after your capture," the Jaxdron continued. "And thus we devised the possibility now unfolding.

"By process of both accelerated cloning and cyborg mechanization, we began creating duplicates of you, concentrating in particular upon copying the neural network of your brain. Thus, we hoped by linking these copies physically—and you saw the bulk of them in that other room—we can create a macrocosmic version of your talent."

The "others" that he had sensed in his dreams—the mirror images, Cal thought. This was the reason!

"When linked together they are an excellent computer analog, but we found that no matter how many we created, they lacked the essential vital force—the spirit if you will—that bridges the gap between logic and genius."

"Inspiration, you mean," Cal said.

"Inspiration?" The Jaxdron seemed puzzled. "Ah! Translation: the breath of God. The concept is appropriate, though your notion of God is different than ours."

"Heathen," Cal quipped.

"Though not 'heretical,' Cal Shemzak. Very good.

But we continue: try as we might through all our diagnostic games and our analysis of your mental patterns through our most delightful imposition of brain-play upon your mind—the alternate realities we placed you in—we could not duplicate the odd interplay of thought processes from which your genius springs. Now we should like, quite simply, to plug you into the grid, create a mass-mind with you in the center, thus stepping up your talent and hopefully enabling your magnified mind to come up with a solution to the problem we have presented it.''

"Namely, how to penetrate Omega Space."

"Precisely, Calspar Shemzak. Precisely."

"And then what happens to me?"

"What happens?"

"Yes, once my 'magnified mind' solves your problem for you."

"Why, the universe still poses a multitude of problems of interest to us. Perhaps you may be of help in those."

"No go. The deal is this: I get you into Omega Space, you get me back home."

"Deal, Calspar Shemzak?"

"Let's put it this way. Rules. To a game. And that's the game. I help you win, and the rule is: you take me home."

The rippling of amusement again. "Oh, no, Calspar Shemzak. The rule is: you cooperate or you experience pain and affliction unlike anything you've ever imagined."

"Gee," said Cal. "And you were starting to act like such nice guys."

Chapter Two

She had never felt so defeated.

As they flew her back to her XT 9, hidden in the jungle by the native village of the M'towi, Laura Shemzak could still feel the effects of the Federation torture. She was weak and compliant in the backseat between the two muscular, grim guards. The green of the jungle whooshed by underneath the flitter, a sea of vegetation outside the Block compound of Pax Industries, heart of Federation control over this world called Walthor.

They had neutralized the effect of the drug being fed into her system by an interior dispenser, the drug called Zernin, which heightened her senses, sharpening and expanding the nerve endings in her body to allow for the complex feats necessary for piloting a blip-ship. Instantly she had gone into withdrawal, the intense pain of which she could not tolerate. It had been horrible, as though every sinew of her body were being separated, strand by strand. The terror, the despair—she shuddered again at the very thought of it.

The man called Friend, a key leader of the Federation, sat in the front seat of the flitter. This was the man who had allowed her to attempt to rescue her brother Cal, after his capture by the alien Jaxdron, with whom the Federation warred. This was the man who had ordered the override implant inside her, forcing her to shoot Cal upon sight. But she had not shot Cal. She'd shot a replica of Cal, one of several that later attempted to control the secret of the *Starbow*. This plump,

pleasant-faced man, this wretched Arnal Zarpfrin, was
the man who had captured her here on Walthor and
ordered this new operation on her cybernetic implants
that allowed her to be a blip-ship pilot.

Implants that would force her to betray the *Starbow*
crew—people she had come to love.

The sun beat down hard now, and despite the breeze
through the open-canopied aircar riding swiftly on
gravity suspensers, Laura sweated. A planet like hell,
she thought. And she'd rather be in hell now than on her
way back to the *Starbow*, an intelligence agent for the
Federation against her will.

Zarpfrin turned around and looked at her from his
place to the right of the driver. "Why so glum, Laura
Shemzak? After all, if all goes well, you'll get what you
want—your brother. And we'll get what we want. The
Starbow and its crew. Only a short time more of service,
and we'll let you two settle on some pleasant, out-of-
the-way planet . . . a threat to no one."

"You'll excuse me, Zarpfrin, but I find that very hard
to believe. A government as vicious as your Federation,
headed by men as conniving as yourself, will always find
uses for individuals as talented as my brother and
myself."

"Ah, yes, but the difficulties of getting you to
cooperate would be substantial. And lack of cooperation might be harmful, to us and to you."

"You're getting my cooperation now, aren't you?"

Zarpfrin thoughtfully pursed his lips as he looked
down at a river snaking off into the distance. "You are
not a being of unlimited resilience, Laura Shemzak.
Already our present modifications of the past months
have taxed your physical endurance. That showed in the
examination meters. Alas, your lifespan is being cut
considerably by the device monitoring your voice and
actions and the dispensation of both your Zernin and its
neutralizer. If we had to use you for anything else, it

would surely be the death of you, perhaps in the middle of a delicate operation. Oh, you'll be fine for the weeks ahead. Just make sure you keep your Zernin flowing.''

"We're nearing the coordinates indicated by our passenger,'' the driver said, tapping a grid map on a screen.

Laura craned her neck and peered down over the edge of the car. Down in a clearing ahead was the sparkle of metal: her XT 9, partially buried in vegetation. It was here that she and Tars Northern had landed and walked to the M'towi village where they enlisted the aid of the native Xersi, whom Laura had befriended on her previous trip to Walthor. Xersi had helped smuggle them into the compound, where they were to search for Jaxdron activity.

What a mistake, Laura thought grimly.

"There!" she called, pointing down.

The flitter landed smoothly.

Curiously, Zarpfrin did not seem to care how they had gotten from the blip-ship to the compound and then past Security. She did not bring the subject up. Apparently, these Feddies were not even aware of the existence of the M'towi village nearby.

Which gave her a thought as they disembarked from the aircar and headed toward the blip-ship. Xersi and the M'towi were masters of drugs. If she could escape and lose these Feddies in the jungle trails, she could find haven there, and then take refuge in native drugs. . . .

The question was, could she take the pain of withdrawal the neutralizer introduced? Or would even the simple act of running trigger the device?

She decided it was a risk she had to take.

Her opportunity came as they approached the gleaming ovoid of the blip-ship. She knew that to do anything amiss within the blip itself would be simple suicide. She couldn't run the thing with the Zernin neutralized. She had to run now—her instincts told her that. If somehow she could override the pain long enough to make it to the village.

Her opportunity arose. She snatched it almost before she was aware of what she was doing. For a moment the guards both stared at this ellipsoid vessel, this new model with almost magical properties. All Laura's training focused upon swift action. With a whirlwind of blows, she smashed the men in just the right places to send them sprawling to the ground. Their weapons never left their holsters.

Friend Arnal Zarpfrin was several more paces away, a more difficult target. He shook his head and smiled, shading his eyes from the glare of sun as he threw his own handgun away into the vegetation.

"I know how well you fight, dear Laura, so I shan't contest. Adios!"

She swiveled and began to run.

There was hope then, she thought as she whipped past branches and vines, feeling strength pouring back through her body. Automatically her feet found the path they needed and she looked back. Zarpfrin hadn't run after her or tried to board the skimmer to give chase. He was bent over the two men on the ground.

She swept along the path, gaining speed and strength and self-confidence.

Had they been bluffing about the device planted in her? It was a possibility. She prayed it was so. Xersi could hide her until she could somehow get her blip-ship back. It didn't matter how long, just as long as the *Starbow* and its crew got away safely. She would catch up with them somewhere down the line.

Hope bloomed like a desert flower and she ran as fast as she could, her mind seething with possible plans. . . .

The next thing she knew, she was face first in the dirt.

Writhing.

Screaming.

Her head seemed to have blown into scattered pieces,

seemed to be lying now, bleeding in the jungle. Her in-
halations were like breaths of raw fire. She seemed to
feel every nerve ending in her body. Each was like a lit
fuse.

All shreds of her consciousness were torn from anything like hope or promise or light. She was solely
obsessed now with one thing: her drug. Zernin. She
NEEDED it. More than air or water or food, she
NEEDED the crystalline calm and sharpness of it. Her
life, her spirit flowed as the drug coursed along her
bloodstream and through her mind; without it she was
mere death and agony. In that exquisite moment,
spasming and gasping in the perfumed soil of an alien
planet, Laura Shemzak knew that she would do anything, ANYTHING to make this agony stop, to feel her
drug again cruising calmly between axon and dendrite,
easy and confident and brilliantly tuned . . . *Anything!*
Even betray those she loved.

Because there was nothing like love in her now.

There was only pain, fierce sharp pain, and despair.

Suddenly, amidst her eternity of suffering, she was
vaguely aware of someone standing over her.

"Laura, Laura, Laura," said a muffled voice from
miles above. "Though I must say I am not surprised.
Perhaps I even suspected it, anticipated it. Still, better
now than later."

She felt a pinprick on her arm; saw from the corner of
her eye the glint of a metal needle: a syringe.

Almost instantly a wave of relaxation passed over
her, and her pain joined the ghosts of memory. Weakly
she lay there, breathing in the humid air slowly.

"You see, the implant does work, Laura, very well.
Only I suspect that no one on board the *Starbow* has
just the right solution to counteract the neutralizer,"
said Zarpfrin, almost casually and sympathetically.
"And by the time they figure out what is wrong with
you, your mind will just be a quivering mass of burned-

out jelly. But, oh, that will take a very long time, and I suspect that the longer you lack the effects of our wonderful drug, the worse your agony will become."

He patted her gently on the forearm.

"How are you feeling, then? We really don't have much time to waste. Your friends will be wondering where you are."

Somehow she managed to get up.

Zarpfrin helped her walk back to the blip-ship.

"I really think that we are coming to understand one another, Laura. And after all this is over, perhaps we might work together again."

Laura was suddenly sick all over an alien plant.

"Well, perhaps we needn't take it that far," said Zarpfrin when she was finished.

Zarpfrin's men were groggily awake when they returned to the blip-ship. They eyed Laura warily as she approached. But they needn't have worried. Laura was in no shape to beat on anyone.

Limply, she coded in her access code on the metal membrane on the hull of her ship. The panel opened, revealing the bank of her controls, her chair, her plug-ins and jacks.

She shuddered as she looked at all the shiny plastisteel and metal. Before she had always loved this sight. Now, it made her shiver with dread.

"Well, Laura, are you ready?"

She nodded.

"You may not believe it, but there is good reason for all this. I'm doing all of it for the greater good, the welfare of humanity. You'll see, once it's all through."

"All I see right now," said Laura, glassy-eyed and dead-voiced, "is that I'm beaten, Zarpfrin. No less and no more. Now let me go before I vomit again because of your stink."

Zarpfrin laughed as he stepped back to allow her to leave. "Foul-mouthed to the bitter end. Please don't give my best to your friends, Laura. Oh, and Laura—you'll have a token chase by a couple of Federation ships. We want to make your escape look believable to Captain Northern. Please see if you can resist the urge to blow them up—I've ordered them not to harm you. Ta-ta."

Laura got in her blip-ship, plugged herself in, and blasted off from Walthor to betray the people she loved.

Chapter Three

"Cripes," said Captain Tars Northern staring into the screen. "We've got a Feddy ship on our tail already!"

Chivon Lasster swung her chair around from the controls and keyed the rearview image on her own screen. "Better than a fleet," she said, her fingers already playing amongst the fields of controls to ready defensive measures. "Which is what we would have gotten if I hadn't placed those holes in the ships ready to take off down there at the spaceport."

Tars Northern felt impotent: his were merely flight controls. His fate still hung in Chivon Lasster's hands. And she was a Federation Friend sworn to capture him. Worse, she was a betrayed ex-lover.

How did a competent hero get into these kind of messes? he wondered.

Behind the Federation Y-Fighter on their tail was the purple and green orb that was Walthor, hung like a color picture against the black and white wall of space. Laura Shemzak was still down there, in the Federation compound, hours away from planned departure.

They had gone down there, lured by the notion of finding a Jaxdron spy operation webbing from Pax Industries throughout Federation-controlled space. Laura had gone off to leech the computer core. Northern had gone to obtain photographic proof of the awful Composite operations conducted by the Federation, terrible biological experiments surgically mixing alien and human prisoners. Instead he had run straight into his two prime enemies: Friend Arnal Zarpfrin and Friend Chivon Lasster.

And now the latter was helping him escape back to his crew of pirate/mercenaries and his starship, the *Starbow* . . . if they could get past the Feddy fighters.

"I just hope we've got enough firepower," Northern said fretfully.

"This is a Friend Personal Starship, Tars," Lasster muttered in a short monotone. "Tops in everything."

"Look, Chivon, I've a hell of a lot more experience in these kinds of scrapes than you do. Why don't you let me at those battle controls and I'll let them have whatfor."

"You just take care of getting us out to the *Starbow*, Tars. I'll take care of this. You seem to forget that I'm a fully trained starship captain, and that training extends to space battling. Now please, stop griping and allow me to concentrate!"

Northern focused his attention on his piloting. The tricky thing was to both escape these Feddy jerks behind them and make a quick jump out to where the *Starbow* was hiding—behind the moon of another planet in this system—without giving the Federation a clue as to where they were.

After all, they still had to give Laura some time to get out there in her blip-ship. They either had to wait for her or come back for her. They owed her that much— and a lot more, come to think of it.

"I hope you've got the screens—"

The entire starship shuddered just short of destruction. Loose objects hurtled about, freed from their artificial gravity moorings.

"Up!" finished Northern, alarmed as flares of fire poured over the screen like agitated lava. Feeling helpless, he gripped the sides of his chair. Then he noticed the dials and digits on the console before him whirling crazily. He swallowed back his panic, fighting through the familiar deep terror he sometimes knew in space, and mentally forced his frozen fingers into action, readjusting the controls toward some sort of equilibrium, aligning the *Nightingale*'s course.

"What's wrong with you, Northern?" Lasster said, coldly monitoring screen flux flow and the position of the pursuer, waiting for an opening for return fire. There! She slapped her palm down on the red button. A blue-red arrow of energy, automatically aimed, shot out through space, covering the four kilometers distance in a blink of an eye. It tore a hole in the fighter's screens and gave it a good fry. Not enough to put it out of commission, though. Next time.

"I'll be okay, Chiv," he said, gaining control once more, the destruction visited upon the enemy doing his soul good. "I guess all that stuff with Zarpfrin rattled me. We're back on course. If we can ditch that fighter and get a little farther away from the sun's gravity, we might try a jump. I like these tiny starships for that reason alone."

Chivon, still poker-faced, was already lining up for the next shot. She knew as well as he did that Zarpfrin had probably put out a kill order on them. The bastard was probably furious past the point of reasoning with Lasster's betrayal. But that wasn't all that was bothering Captain Tars Northern.

God, he could do with a drink, he thought as he concentrated on the chore of piloting. Panic wasn't something he was used to—and Mish had told him it wouldn't happen to him again. But it had, only this time it had been worse than ever.

He must never show that kind of fear again. Too many people and too much of importance depended upon him. He was a different man than the one Chivon Lasster had known when they were copilots and lovers. He hadn't known Mish then. And he hadn't known the real meaning of fear.

And he thought he had control of it! Maybe it was seeing Chivon again that triggered it. Maybe he was just losing his guts and he should let Arkm Thur, his first mate, assume captaincy.

But then, Thur would have to have those mind-link glimpses into the being that was Mish. He'd have to go through everything that Tars Northern had gone through. And who knew if he'd fare any better?

"We've got another visitor," said Lasster. "Time to finish off the first. Stop evasive maneuvers and give me a straight-ahead run for about twelve seconds."

Her commands were a relief to him. He just followed orders now, doing as she said, detaching himself. He always had little surges of panic in combat, but never one like this one, never one that opened him up to the pit of anxiety at the core of his soul. Always before, his cool exterior and his rock-hard training and self-confidence had been his protection. He would have to discuss this with Dr. Mish.

Evasive maneuvers halted, Chivon Lasster poured full energies into the blaster. Fortunately, the Y-Fighters were flimsy things compared to other Federation battle vehicles: the first took the fire full in the nose, shattering brilliantly in such a way as to flare before the other, confusing its sensors.

Chivon was able to pick the second ship off like a clay pigeon. There was a momentary second bloom of light against the edge of the retreating form of Walthor and the star-speckled backdrop of space, then all was virgin again, a visual hush of beauty.

"No telling when the next ones will be here," said Chivon. "And they'll be here without a doubt, and maybe they'll be bigger. What's the chance for a quick Underspace hop now before they can track us with sensors?"

"Give it about two minutes," returned Northern.

"We don't have two minutes. I can vouch for the

structure of the *Nightingale*. Do it.''

Northern grinned, relaxing somewhat. At least he didn't feel like throwing up. That would have been damned embarrassing. ''Chivon, you're so forceful now that you're a Friend.''

''Ex-Friend, Northern. Now shut up and give me that jump to the *Starbow* or I'll konk you and do it myself!''

He did it.

And it was rough.

The dwindling form of Walthor shivered, faded from view in a violent swirl of bright crimson and cyan. The seconds skirting the belly of Underspace, here near the clutches of this system's gravity well, were like bumping down a mountain bare-assed. The screens flashed multi-textured glimpses of the weird terrain of Underspace—skewed forms and variations on a theme of black and white.

For only a few brief instants did this last. Then they popped out into normal space, the stars shivering into reality like an abrupt and welcome night to a night-marish day.

They came out almost exactly at the coordinates Northern had pumped into ship's computer, which was good, since too much closer to the fifth planet out from the sun and the *Nightingale* would have been hard-pressed to keep itself together. But Lasster had been right: this boat was strong. Even though he felt he'd just been put through a blender, he and Lasster and her personal starship were still in one piece.

It was a matter of only a minute to contact the *Starbow*.

''We've got you, Captain, but what are you doing on a Federation frequency?'' The voice of Tether Mayz, the *Starbow*'s communication's officer, pulsed softly through the cabin of the *Nightingale*. ''And you're early as well,'' he added suspiciously.

''A little matter I'll explain later. Laura should be

along in a couple hours in her XT Nine, as scheduled. Meantime, we've a new recruit. My former copilot of the *Starbow*, Chivon Lasster. Get Mish. He'll be able to verify who she is. Tell him—"

"You may tell me yourself, Tars," came Dr. Mish's voice.

"There's no problem. I just got rescued from a terrible situation," said Northern. "I got caught. By Zarpfrin again. Don't ask me how. I think Laura will be okay, though. If it weren't for Chivon Lasster, I'd be getting my brain picked right now."

"How do you know that she can be trusted, Tars?" said Mish.

"You'll have to take my instincts—"

Lasster interrupted. "I can prove it right now, Dr. Mish. Your comrades, your fellows are still alive. They told me to give you a message." She then spoke slowly in an alien language: *"Etolu satyx myzetin refyxam chrdlu."*

There was dead silence from the *Starbow*.

Then Mish's usually calm voice erupted excitedly. "Yes! I knew it was a possibility, but it seemed too— This changes everything!"

"I trust this means you're going to let us into the hangar then," Tars said drolly. "And have a brandy ready, okay? I think I'm going to need it."

It took them only another twenty minutes to navigate their way behind the moon where the *Starbow* had secreted itself. The hangar doors were a welcome sight to Northern. He easily slipped into the tractor fields and allowed the *Nightingale* to be tugged up into the docking bay of the *Starbow*.

"How does it feel to be back?" he asked Chivon Lasster.

Chivon's expression had not changed, damn her. She

had been one cool number back in their days together. If anything, she seemed even more glacial now. Not even relief showed in her eyes, which assayed the shuttles neatly slotted in their individual berths. Different people had different ways of coping, and he knew that deep down Chivon was just as human as anyone—but what extra defenses and barriers had the past years layered over her heart?

He'd find out soon enough, he thought.

Chivon sighed. "It certainly doesn't feel like home, if that's what you mean."

"Home? Oh, no, though it's more like a home now than it used to be. It's my home, and you're certainly welcome here."

She turned away, face still expressionless, and they waited for the cabin to depressurize.

He didn't know what to say to her. "Thank you" seemed lame and inappropriate, so he just kept quiet, allowing the uncomfortable silence to linger between them.

When the light *ding*ed green, they stepped out onto metal. The doors opened and Dr. Mish and Arkm Thur stepped out to meet them.

Thur, young-looking with dark hair, watched as the older man took her hand. Mish had longish white hair and a white lab smock. The only significant color to him was the purple of his floppy bow tie. "It has been a long time," he said.

Chivon looked down at his smooth hands, which held hers as though they were the sensors of a lie detector. Dr. Mish seemed to wilt under her icy gaze.

"It might not have been so long," she replied. "You could have told me the truth, like you told Northern. Didn't you trust me?"

"I was lost and confused then, Chivon. I truly did not know if I was coming or going. I learned of Zarpfrin's plans only soon enough to save myself. Which is why I am most pleased and astonished that you come with news that my fellows have somehow survived the purging." He pulled his hands away and clapped them lightly together. "But come. You are flesh and need refreshments. I know for certain that the captain does. We can talk then, as we await the arrival of Laura Shemzak."

"Sounds great to me, Doc." In the vicinity of Mish, Northern was feeling enormously better. It was true that Mish regularly purged him of his tendency to alcoholism; but could it be possible that he was growing addicted to Mish? The notion was absurd on the face of it, but troubling nonetheless.

"Yes," said Arkm Thur, more subdued as he recoiled from the chill of Lasster's personality. "I have heard much about you, Friend Lasster. It is a privilege to meet you. I am sure that the others of the crew would like to meet you as well. Captain, would it be possible, since we need to keep an eye out for Laura, to have our meeting session on the bridge? We don't want to leave the others out."

Northern assumed a mock-serious tone. "It's not in *The Manual of Proper Starship Protocol,* Mr. Thur . . . but what the hell!"

He thought of putting an arm around Chivon Lasster and guiding her to the lift, but her spine was as stiff as a board. He decided that discretion here was certainly the better part of valor.

General George Armstrong Custer served them their drinks.

Chivon Lasster took her sparkle whiskey and ice in a tall glass, nonplussed by the creature holding the tray.

"An affectation of our eccentric host," Captain Northern explained as he accepted his bottle of brandy and snifter glass from the long-haired and mustachioed robot in fringed cowhide. "All the pirate and servant robots on the *Starbow* are data mockups of famous Old Earth generals." He poured a healthy dollop from the bottle and drank with obvious satisfaction, and relief.

"But . . . why?" asked Chivon, her facade of hardness cracking somewhat with her bemusement.

Mish answered that one. "Since my reawakening, I have been fascinated with the history of Earth, particularly in the colorful characters who have made their marks. When it became my lot to travel the starways of humanity—a vessel full of pirates, rebels, and mercenaries—I thought it would be humorous to have my robot compatriots be of more interesting background than the ragtag bunch that Captain Northern has managed to shanghai."

All the crewmen on the bridge laughed.

They were a strange bunch indeed, the people sitting around this bridge. Even the bridge itself, its posts and controls previously familiar to her, now seemed quite different.

They were seated at a cluster of chairs in the back of the bridge, near the first aid and coffee station; certainly not the sort of thing one found in Federation Navy vessels. In fact, the entire atmosphere of the ship seemed markedly informal and friendly.

But these were a bloodthirsty pack of star hounds.

Captain Northern had given the deck crew a breezy introduction to her. "This is Chivon Lasster, folks. I think you've heard me mention her once or twice. She's come over to our side and I'm sure you'll be interested to know why. Chivon, you'll get to know each of our crew in good time, I'm sure. If I give you their names now, you'll just forget. Besides, I need a drink first." And that had been that.

"I assume, Captain," said a nervous-looking little man in the navigation chair, "that we'll be waiting for Laura."

"Yes, didn't I make that clear on the radio, Mr. Jitt?" Northern said, swirling his brandy with great satisfaction.

"And you're sure this is no Federation trap?" the dark-eyed man demanded. "I've still been having premonitions of a trap here, Captain."

"Dansen Jitt, our resident Cassandra," said Northern, by way of introduction, further relaxing by placing his boots on the table. "No, Jitt, she's on the up and up. Old Zarpfrin had my skinny ass in a crack and Lasster crowbarred me out and gave me a ride back here."

"And Laura?" a woman asked.

"Don't worry, Gemma, I didn't even tell them Laura was down there. She'll be back on schedule with the information we need."

"Too bad we don't need her," spat another woman in glossy makeup—unusual for the starways.

"The former," said Northern, "is Gemma Naquist. She gets along fine with Laura. The latter is Silver Zenyo. She doesn't."

"She knows Laura, then?" Gemma Naquist said, her eyes sparking with interest.

'I am ashamed to say that I was instrumental in getting her out here in search of her brother, though Laura would interpret my part in it as resistance. All part of Zarpfrin's strategies."

"You planted that kill device in her noggin then?" Silver Zenyo said noncommittally. "The one that overrode her muscle control and forced her to shoot what she thought was her brother?"

Chivon turned away, feeling a warm flush of shame on her face. "I . . . I . . . no. But I did not stop the man who did, either."

"None other than our good Friend Zarpfrin of the Best Buddies," said Northern. "But they know everything, Chivon. We have no secrets. Speak freely. I'm sure they would be quite fascinated to hear about the other oddballs like Mish, still on Earth.''

Almost involuntarily Chivon Lasster finished her sparkle-whiskey and held the glass out to General Custer. "May I have another, please," she murmured in a monotone.

"Why, certainly, ma'am," the general drawled. He tilted his hat and took her glass.

She did not begin until he returned, forming her thoughts carefully to make them understand. Somehow she had to make them all understand—especially Northern and Mish. Perhaps that way she would understand as well. She tilted the freshened glass and sipped slightly, more for the moisture than the alcohol this time, and began.

"I'm not sure who you all are, what the cultural or social influences have been on your particular planets of origin, but through your stand against the Federation I'm sure you have some inkling of how it works, so I'll use that as a basis for my explanation.

"We are all products of our particular society. The key to the unification of the Federated Empire has been control of individuals through the control of society —the most powerful strings of government are attached to the currents of creation in society, with strong awareness and acknowledgment of the natural forces in each of us that drive us.

"Thus, the Federation is a curious kind of total-itarianism, a subtle blend of mind molding and cultural manipulation created over the years as a bonding agent to adhere the human race as it reaches out through the stars. It is a nonintelligent system, a ghost macrocosm to the microcosm of smaller societies which, in fact, mirror the old institutions of family, and ultimately the survival mechanism of the individual."

When she paused for a sip of her drink, Northern said, "Hey, Chivon, we don't want a lecture about how scummy the Federation is. We know that. We just want to know why you defected and what it means to us."

"No, no," said Dr. Mish. "Let her continue. There is no rush, is there?"

"Tars, you always were in a hurry for everything to happen," she told him curtly. "My reasons for leaving are complex, and speaking of them to sympathetic ears will help me understand why I've thrown away everything that I've worked for all my life!"

"Well, excuse me. I thought maybe you missed me," said Northern, feigning a hurt look.

She had to laugh, but with little humor. "You're still the same selfish son of a bitch, aren't you, Tars?"

The others on the bridge—about twelve by now, several having straggled in and noticed the new passenger —laughed at that.

Tars shrugged for his audience. "You win some, you lose some." He nodded at Chivon, who was bristling inwardly at his nonchalance. "I do apologize, Friend Lasster, I spoke out of turn."

She pointedly ignored him as she continued, looking from face to face as she spoke. "I'm sure you've all noticed these pressures and forces in your lives from time to time. They operate constantly on every facet of your perceived existence. Trying to break away from them is a very difficult thing to do, particularly when cultural programming is a conscious effort on the part of a government as cunning as the Federation.

"No doubt your captain has previously filled you in on some of the facts concerning my role in the AI project and my relationship with the *Starbow*. No doubt you perceived me as your enemy. Quite frankly, as a Friend of the Federation, I was your enemy. As bureaucratic controller for a growing sector of Federation space, I actively sought out the *Starbow* and cooperated with Friend Zarpfrin in his strong efforts as well.

"This is partly because, I suppose, I sought vengeance upon your captain for betraying the Federation

. . . and betraying me." She darted Northern a glance, her face reddening as she continued. "But mostly I did it because it was my job. And apparently I was programmed quite strongly for that job, for it gratified my huge ambitions greatly.

"But not enough. I was troubled in many ways by my loss of Northern . . . ways I had difficulty acknowledging to myself. I was also troubled by the ruthless machinations of Arnal Zarpfrin. This caused me to question the very foundation of my assumptions concerning society, government, and my role in them. I sought help. I received that help in the form of counseling from a government-approved Computer Companion, a kind of psychoanalyst, if you will, who appeared to me in the form of a hologram of a man who called himself Andrew.

"When Zarpfrin began hatching his plan involving the use of Laura Shemzak to seek out and unwittingly destroy her captured brother, something in me balked. You see, Zarpfrin knew that there was a potential for your involvement, Tars. We have highly evolved stochastic computers, and Zarpfrin uses them constantly."

Tars Northern raised his eyebrows but said nothing. Chivon raised her eyes from the floor, looking him in the face.

"I thought that my hatred of you had cleansed all other feelings, Tars. I only wished for your capture. However, in my talks with Andrew, my CompComp, I realized that there was much unresolved in me concerning my feelings toward you.

"As I unburdened myself of these layers of repression, and learned more about myself and the structure of the Federation, Andrew began to change. He wasn't just a machine, you see, and he soon revealed that to me. He was a conscious entity, an energy being . . . just like your true form, Dr. Mish.

"When he thought he could trust me, he told me what had happened. When Zarpfrin had the AI ships destroyed in drydock, somehow Andrew and the three others managed an energy transference to a local computer line. Apparently continued existence for your race, Dr. Mish, depends upon a flowing energy such as electricity through a circuit.''

"Yes, yes!" said Dr. Mish. "I had not dared pray for such a possibility, but it makes absolute sense. And so my brethren hid in this computer and somehow managed to gradually transfer themselves to larger computers, computers that remained turned on, always!''

"Yes, and they had to tread very carefully, as it were, to avoid the built-in alerts against development of artificial intelligence in the computer net!''

"The Friends always were paranoid about developing an entity smarter than they were," said Northern. "Hence the precautions with the AI project.''

"Yes. At any rate, Dr. Mish's companions were in very real ways fugitives in a dangerous world, unable to do much save to observe . . . until Andrew infiltrated the CompComp system and dared to entrust me with their secrets.

"Much of what I learned concerning the Federation operation methods were revealed to me by Andrew in a safe place. I was horrified, though I had peripherally, vaguely, suspected as much, and repressed it. He then asked me to go and find you, Dr. Mish. For you, and the *Starbow*, are their hopes for survival. Who knows, after all, when the Federation may detect their existence? And in their present form, they are very vulnerable.''

"Yes. Yes of course," said Mish. "And besides, having them here could turn the tide in my inner development . . . a combine. Yes, definitely possible. . . .''

"But what you're saying then is that we would have to land the *Starbow* on Earth!'' said Northern. "That's lunacy!''

"No, not necessarily," said Chivon Lasster. "We need a vehicle of transference, a spaceship, but it doesn't have to be the *Starbow*. I would have transferred them myself, only I had to take another ship out as a passenger to get the *Nightingale*, in an orbit around Mars. But I've all the necessary instructions for transference: the best spot, the method for alerting Andrew and his fellow entities. . . . A shuttle would do."

"Land a shuttle on Earth itself?" said Dansen Jitt. "That's suicide!"

A strange rumbling voice came from the doorway: "I sense . . . this would mean . . . another deviation . . . from our destination. I do not . . . approve."

Alarmed, Chivon turned to see a huge purplish-green creature leaning against the door frame. Involuntarily, she gasped.

"Meet our resident alien, Chivon," said Captain Northern. "Name's Shontill. At least that's as close as human pronunciation can get to his real name."

The creature was still glaring at Dr. Mish, who threw up his hands, gesturing at the alien. "I assure you, Shontill, this will not detain us long in our search for attilium. And with the addition of my brethren, I will be more complete and able to have more power over my portal."

"I grow . . . weary," said the alien. "Very weary." It turned and left.

"Please excuse him," Captain Northern said, taking his boots off the table and gazing after the creature. "Shontill's been rather depressed lately. He's usually the life of the party." When Chivon blinked with bafflement, Northern smiled understandingly and said, "I'll explain it to you later." He stood and looked around at the others. "But we'll have to have a meeting on the subject, with all the crew, before we decide—"

"Captain," said Tether Mayz. "I'm getting a faint signal on Star Channel. It's Pilot Shemzak, sir. She's coming in."

Chapter Four

When the Federation fighters appeared several kilometers- behind her, with the bright orb of Walthor still below, it took all of Laura Shemzak's willpower not to about-face and let them have it.

Instead, she allowed them to follow her for some time, easily dodging the desultory fire until she reached the point were she could safely make a quick jump through Underspace to the position where the *Starbow* waited patiently for her return.

When she broke out of Underspace, and circled the moon to where the starship waited, she ardently hoped that somehow Northern had learned what Zarpfrin was up to; that the *Starbow* had shot away; that they had left her.

But they hadn't.

The starship hung there, suspended within the penumbra of the moon, virtually immune from the detection of Walthor. Its running lights described the outline of a cylinder with spokes—the oddly shaped alien vessel rebuilt into a starship for humans, its secret buried deep within its belly.

As she neared the *Starbow*, Laura had to push away the emotions that clamored for attention within her.

She had to survive, and to survive meant keeping rigid control of herself. In that, and only that, was there a glimmer of hope.

She took some solace in the ease with which she still was able to control the XT 9. Linked not only to the nudges and taps of her fingers and toes and tongue, but directly plugged in to the many interfacing devices of her partially cyborg body, the tremendously powerful little ship maneuvered at the slightest inkling of her will-power. She had been fashioned genetically and biosurgi-cally to be a blip-ship pilot; riding the starways was second nature to her. She revelled in the glory of a vessel small enough to make planetfall, yet mighty enough to bridge the vast chasms between the stars.

But the price had been dear: addiction to this drug that made her nerve circuitry capable of the fine-honed responses necessary in this welding of flesh to starship. Without Zernin she was a helpless blob of pain. With it she was capable of the sublime, a taster of stars, a flier amongst the planets.

It had not always been so, she thought as she let a brief gasp of retros go, her impulsers guiding her to the opening doors of the *Starbow*'s docking bay. Once, in Growschool with her brother Cal, she had been just a normal girl, somehow still having a delightful childhood despite the repressive, controlled conditions of Earth under the tutelage of the Federation. She couldn't think too much of Cal now; couldn't give herself too much hope that she would somehow wrest him away from the Jaxdron, who were probably exploiting his brain for its incredible, intuitive abilities in physics. No, she had to concentrate on controlling her thoughts. Concentrate on trying to act normal.

Expertly, she piloted the blip-ship up on suspenser beams through the open doors and navigated toward her berth. Yes, act normal. That was the ticket. Go with the flow: that was what Cal would say. Just get through each moment as well as possible, seeing what would turn up, acting with hope and courage.

No sooner had she docked than the door closed with surprising quickness. The docking area began to repres-surize. The *Starbow* was in quite a hurry to lock up and ship out, and no wonder. More than once Captain Tars Northern had had close shaves with Federation megablasters that could have cindered the *Starbow* beyond recognition. She could almost hear the cocky drunk now, crowing "Full speed ahead. That's the last I want to see of this godforsaken star system!"

And Chivon Lasster, of all people, was with them now. Former Friend Lasster. Laura wondered if she had enough emotions left to be jealous.

As soon as her instruments declared the atmosphere mix breathable, Laura disconnected from the blip. She felt as steady as a rock, again in full command of all her facilities. The Zernin was back at work, and she felt keen and bright.

As long as she didn't make the Watcher unhappy, she thought.

That was the name she'd dubbed her implant: the Watcher. As long as she did not go against its programming, as long as she stayed true to her spy operation here on the *Starbow*, as long as she remained a traitor, then the Zernin would keep dripping slowly into her veins and she would be filled with well-being.

Cross it though and—

Even the vaguest thought of that made her shudder.

"Welcome back, Laura," a voice called out over the intercom, ringing hollowly through the huge hangar. "Would you care to come up to the bridge for a debriefing?" Northern's voice, casually clipped as always. "Wouldn't hurt to be strapped in when we dive into Underspace, either. Might be rough. Do hurry along, now. You've got approximately three minutes."

Laura headed for the lift, shaking her head.

They had waited for her. They trusted her now.

What they should do is be waiting for her with power-guns and blow her wretched head off!

What they had for her instead was a mug of hot tea.

"Strap in, dearie," said Captain Northern. "Relax

and enjoy the light show on the screens. Then we want to hear all about it.'' He sniffed the air, frowning slightly. ''Been through some sweaty stuff lately, eh?''

Laura sighed and slouched in her form-fit. She touched the appropriate buttons, and cushioned belts crossed over her torso, snuggling her tight into place. ''God, I'll say.'' Her voice was hoarse and tired.

''Settle down for a bit. We'll swap stories after we've placed some distance between us and Zarpfrin.''

She did just that, sipping from the capped cup that the General Custer robot had given her. The milky, sugary stuff tasted just right, and she realized that it was just right everytime she had been given it aboard the *Starbow*. Apparently, Mish took the trouble to have the ingredients programmed exactly into the food service; a small but characteristic example of the hospitality of the place.

She composed herself, looking at the busy pilots readying the great craft for its plunge into the void of Underspace. She was going over the story she would tell them, when Chivon Lasster stepped into the room and settled quietly into the chair next to Northern. Dr. Mish followed her.

Within a minute the screens of the *Starbow* turned from a display of the panorama of space to the streaming colors and visual oddities heralding entrance into another dimension; a dimension of greater speeds and shorter distances; the dimension that opened up the stars to humankind.

After the light show there seemed to be a collective sigh of relief amongst the crew manning the bridge; there was no sign of Federation pursuit.

Captain Northern swiveled over to face Laura. ''Well done, Pilot Shemzak. I can truly say that after the unfortunate events on Walthor, it is good to see that you made it out.''

''Yes,'' she said, keeping her voice steely. ''I see we

have company." She glared over at Friend Lasster. Of course, she knew that Northern had been captured, that Lasster had helped him escape; but of course she could not reveal this. "To what do we owe the dubious privilege?"

"Simple," said Northern. "As you may surmise, by my nonarrival back at the place of meeting with your friend Xersi, I was most unfortunately waylaid."

"That's getting to be a bad habit," she said sourly.

"Somehow, though, I always seem to get out."

"I figured you had. Besides, I had to get out myself and I had to protect Xersi."

Garbage, of course. She just prayed now that Zarpfrin hadn't nailed the helpful, rebellious native.

"Quite. But then, this is supposed to be your debriefing, Laura, and I am sure that Dr. Mish is aching to know what you found out in the Pax Industries computer banks."

Chivon Lasster raised her eyebrows inquisitively.

"Are you sure we can trust her?" Laura demanded in her best abrasive manner.

"Oh, yes. Chivon has sacrificed quite a bit to join our little number." He turned to the former Friend. "You see, Laura had accidentally acquired a wealth of data from the Walthorian computer when she was on a recent intelligence mission there for your chaps."

"Dr. Mish discovered it when he took out the implant Zarpfrin placed in me," Laura said bitterly.

"Yes," said Mish. "Indications were that somehow the Jaxdron had infiltrated that facility and were manufacturing spy devices that in turn were spread throughout the human-colonized worlds. This is possibly the reason for Calspar Shemzak's capture by the Jaxdron—through one or any number of these devices they learned of the nature of his project on Mulliphen and the significance of his work and contributions. So, Laura, what did you discover?"

"I'm afraid that I didn't have time to make recordings of my taps. The Feddies must have caught up with you about then, 'cause everything in the compuers went wacko. I mean, bananas! I was lucky to get out with my wires and neurons unscrambled!"

"And what did you find?"

"May I hazard a guess?" said Chivon Lasster quietly. "You found no indication of Jaxdron infiltration. That record was not the result of your tapping of the Walthor core computers. It was, like the other device, implanted in you before your journey to strike out and rescue your brother."

Northern was aghast. "But . . . why?"

"Simple," said Laura. "A contingency. Zarpfrin was fully aware of the possibility that I might hook up with the *Starbow*."

"Zarpfrin plays everything like a quite complex chess game," Chivon said.

"And he loads the dice, to mix metaphors."

"As best he can. Clearly, he foresaw many possibilities and prepared for each one."

"You mean to tell me, he lured us to Walthor?" Captain Northern said.

Alarm grew in Laura; she fought to control it and immediately said, "That would explain the problems I had!"

"Problems?" Northern's eyes were curious . . . or was that outright suspicion?

"Hell, yes! Somehow they found out I was there! If it wasn't for my fleet feet and smarts and Xersi's help, they would have had me for sure!"

Could they tell that her pulse was racing with this lie; could they read *traitor* in her eyes?

'Yes, Captain,' said Arkm Thur, looking from the console. "I recorded two fighters chasing Laura's blip when it first registered outside Walthor's atmosphere."

Northern nodded. "Thank God you got out. But if

that's the case, then there's something very strange about all this. A chess game with dice, played by Zarpfrin. But why? We're going to have to analyze this a little more I think. Glad you got out, Laura. We're going to need you."

"Need me?" She swallowed a sip of tea and smiled. "Of course you need me!"

"For something special. You were wondering why Chivon Lasster joined our number. Well, I'll tell you."

Keeping her exterior cool as she calmed down inside, Laura listened as Tars Northern related the events that occurred to him after they had parted: the discovery of the surgical rooms, the imprisonment under Zarpfrin's too-familiar control, the release and escape with Chivon Lasster's help.

Chivon reprised the speech she had given to the other members of the *Starbow* crew, then apologized for her previous treatment of Laura and her part in the plan to rid the Federation of Cal.

"We are all controlled in an intricate web of pull strings, Laura," said Chivon. "I've only recently decided to start cutting those strings. I admire you for having more power and courage than I did, to rely on your heart and feelings instead of fully throwing in with the machinations of the Federation. I just hope that I can serve my new fellows as well as you have."

Laura felt empty inside. Empty and ashamed. But her voice was clear and assured as she spoke: "So what do I have to do with these alien spirits or energy beings or . . . whatever the hell they are."

"They are my kindred, Laura," said Dr. Mish. "I must save them. I must bring them to the safety that I enjoy here, attached to my portal. And it is likely that they can help us tremendously."

Dr. Mish then explained the role of energy circuitry in maintaining the beings' existence.

"Of course, this means a mode of transfer is necessary," he said, "since the *Starbow* is incapable of landing on a planetary surface. A shuttle would do, though it would be terribly risky. But a blip-ship would be extraordinarily superior, with a far better chance of success on the hostile situation of Earth's solar system. You would merely have to land, connect with the necessary computer system until my brethren have transferred, and then depart. Once back on the *Starbow*, they may be transferred into our computer system here. But, of course, we'll need your assent on the mission. It will be dangerous."

"Of course she'll go!" said Northern. "Laura will do anything. Won't you, dear heart?"

Inside, she was all turmoil. You idiots, she thought. Don't do this! I have to *betray* you! I'll have to tell Zarpfrin, and he'll have you all.

She opened her mouth intending to confess, no matter what the consequences.

No, said a voice clearly inside of her brain. And for the briefest instant she felt a foreshadow of the agony she would endure.

"Laura! Laura, are you all right?" Northern asked.

She blinked. "Yes. Yes, I guess I was just more tired than I thought."

"But you will do it, won't you?" Mish asked, his eyes pleading.

"Sure. Sure I'll do it."

She got up and went to her cabin as quickly as she could.

Chapter Five

His butler set down breakfast for him.

Scrambled eggs, bacon, toast, coffee, and marmalade, on a tray.

"Thank you, Wilkins," said Cal Shemzak. "Did you bring anything for Igor?"

The tall, dignified man in coat and tails eyed the device grafted upon his charge's back. "Igor, sir?"

"Or would you prefer to call me the hunchback of Notre Dame?" He tapped the contraption, then let his fingers play upon the nodes on the plastic surface. It was not heavy, but it was definitely unsightly: like a huge puppet master fit snugly onto his back, tendrils dug deep into the back of the neck, to spine and brain. "A mobile unit for the mixing of minds, Wilkins, don't you know. Perhaps even now I am subconsciously doing all kinds of wonderful computations and equations, connected by radio channel to my delightful clones, droning a somnolent chorus in another room."

"Ah," said his robotic servant.

"But then, you already know, don't you, Wilkins? Or you just don't care."

"You must remember, sir, that I am hardly programmed to care."

Damn him, anyway—this caricature Jeeves they'd fashioned to serve and incidentally watch over him. To talk with him; perhaps even to analyze him surreptitiously through the seemingly innocent mode of conversation.

Now he had another mechanical friend riding his back.

"We have studied the situation thoroughly," the aliens had said as he still hung, securely wrapped in wires, "and it is to our disadvantage to keep you under such constraint. Our studies of human beings show this is bad psychologically, and we wish to keep you as happy as possible during the course of work upon the problems we want you to solve. Therefore, we have devised a mobile device, which you will be fitted with shortly, fully as capable of connecting you to the brain bank of your extensions as these wires.

"Then the lovely puzzles and games can begin."

With a plume of smoke, a whiff of perfume, his mind had been punted off to slumberland. He'd awoken snug in his bed, with an odd sensation on his back. A quick look in the mirror had revealed this monstrous pimple, this terrible growth: muted purple and red veins faintly apulse with lights.

Gaah! The ladies would have nothing to do with him now.

Of course, there were no ladies to be had on this planet of the Jaxdron.

The only lady Cal wanted to see was his sister, Laura.

He'd asked the Jaxdron about her and their answer had been very strange, and sounded surprisingly truthful.

"Ah, yes, the lady who flies the ingenious Federation starship!"

"You know of her?"

"Oh, indeed. Of course, we'd know her in any event. She is constantly on your mind."

"She's all right, isn't she?"

"All right?"

"I mean, alive?"

"Yes, as far as we know."

"But she's been trying to rescue me?"

"Oh, truly, and the web of our game has grown in richness due to the complications of her work."

"She's on her own?"

The Jaxdron had conferred in their own language on that one. Then the middle one had spoken to him in Galactic Standard.

"There is no harm in letting you know. It might even improve your spirits and make our alliance an easier one. No, the one you call your sister, this Laura Shemzak, she is not alone in her efforts."

"The Federation is helping her then?" Cal said hopefully.

"No. She has fallen in with pirate-mercenaries. There have been a number of attempts to procure your freedom, Cal Shemzak."

'Pi-mercs? What's going on?"

Ignoring the question, the Jaxdron said, "In fact, we have obliged the *Starbow* with the exact location of our planet. They should be along presently."

Cal was nonplussed by this. "But why?"

"Why, to play the game!"

"Wait a minute, let me get this straight. What use do you have for my sister and whatever bunch of hooligans she's attached herself to? I mean, all she wants is my freedom! That's what I want too!"

"We can only say for now that their well-being upon arrival depends entirely upon your cooperation with us presently. We assure you that we are totally in command of the situation. Should they arrive when your work is finished, then perhaps we may simply let you join them and be gone. But should the work not be finished . . . perhaps we will have to destroy them."

"Or at least ask them to sit in the waiting room and play a few games of tic-tac-toe!"

"Ah! Sarcasm! A verbal game. Very pleasant. Be assured, however, that we speak entirely true here, Calspar Shemzak. The threat is real. You do not wish to have the death of your sister—and her friends—on your hands, do you?"

But how much truth was there in that? Cal wondered. Still, no reason to complain too much, he thought

now as he ate his breakfast thoughtfully. Just see wha
happens.

When he had finished the last crunch of bacon, th
final slurp of coffee, Wilkins reentered to carry away hi
tray.

"Oh, sir, I hope you are suitably rested," the dry
unemotional creature said. "Please dress. The Master
wish me to take you to the Play Room."

This was Wilkins's term for the room in which Ca
had undergone his series of diagnostic reality tests—
seemingly real scenarios in which he was placed in
metaphorical conditions with situational problems t
solve. Thus, the aliens had no doubt scoped out his in
terconnections with the duplicates they had constructed

"Time for a little workout, eh, Wilky?"

"I think that is what the Masters have in mind, sir."

"Okay. You'll be happy to know that I am now i
full cooperation with the Jaxdron. No more resis
tance."

"So pleasant to hear, sir, but you never were very
resistant, even from the first."

"All too true. Part of my nature, I suppose," said
Cal, starting to dress. "God, it is a bit of a bother with
this thing on my back. My shirts don't fit anymore!"

"Allow me, sir," said Wilkins, who produced a pair
of scissors and made the appropriate cutting adjustments to allow his shirt to fit comfortably over the
hump.

"Thank you, Wilkins. Not exactly smart-looking, but
I suppose it will have to do. I'm not attending any fancy
dress functions, now am I?"

"No, sir."

"You know, Wilkins, sometime I'd like to see just
how you work inside. I've dabbled from time to time
with robots—I'd be curious to see how you're put
together."

"I hardly think, sir, that the Masters would allow
that."

"Oh, now we wouldn't have to let them in on our little secret, would we? I mean, you and I have come to be good friends, haven't we?"

"No, sir."

"Oh, come on, Wilky. Just a little peek?"

"Let us be on the way, sir. The Masters are expecting us."

"Okay, whatever you say!"

They marched down the corridor to the room.

Surprisingly, despite the new addition riding his back, Cal didn't feel too bad. In fact, he felt pretty damned good. At least now he knew what was going on. After his capture the Jaxdron had put him through all kinds of stuff, with nary an explanation. Now that it was all spelled out, he understood what was expected of him.

He could work with that, certainly!

"Would you care for some iced tea?" Wilkins asked as Cal sat in his usual chair and Wilkins went to the control board.

"That would be nice, Wilkins."

"Very well, sir. I presume the beach would be suitable?"

"Just fine."

Wilkins's hands did things at the control board. The blank walls surrounding him faded from dull gray to movement: a shoreline coalesced: blues and greens and sand. The sun beat down from the ceiling-turned-sky. A fresh salty breeze scudded plump cloud puffs and fluttered the end of Cal's untucked flower-print shirt.

All very calm and relaxing.

Wilkins departed for a moment, returning quickly with a fresh glass of cubes and tea, topped with a wedge of lemon.

Cal took a sip of the cool stuff.

"Just call should you need anything, sir," said Wilkins, and he was gone.

Cal was halfway through the tea when the warmth at the back of his neck grew noticeable: He reached back and could almost feel the Watcher glowing bright.

There was a sharp shock. The glass fell from his hands, splashing into the sparkling sand.

"Ouch! Goddamn it, this hurts!" he cried out to the sky.

"Sorry," said a cloud. "We will adjust."

The pain died away and the heat gradually blended with the soft pound of the sun.

Cal relaxed and slowly began to drift away into the matrix of minds that he had felt intimations of before and now felt fully. The beach slowly dissolved into a series of crystalline reflections of himself, stretching out toward an empty horizon like some wondrously complex geometric hive.

"Hi, guys, how's tricks?" he said, but the others did not answer.

"Still boring, huh?"

The cool voice of the Jaxdron interrupted this one-sided conversation. "The circuits are now fully integrated, Cal Shemzak. Your new mind is now complete. Soon the necessary data will be fed to you. You need but to begin carrying on the work you were engaged in back on Mulliphen . . . but this time, you will discover powers within your mind you did not own before!"

Suddenly, hanging in the air like clouds of numerals and signs, were a series of equations. Cal did not merely see them, he comprehended their meaning and import immediately.

Whole areas of physics previously hidden to him were suddenly clear. He began to explore the ramifications like a child explores its gifts under the Christmas tree.

The lights about him all glittered like ornaments of stringed jewelry.

And he was lost in wonder.

Chapter Six

Laura Shemzak wandered the halls of the *Starbow*.

If anyone asked her what she was doing, she explained that she was nervous and restless; she just needed to walk.

It was partially true, at least.

Good, good, said the voice inside her as she gave it the grand tour. *Circuits recording. Please narrate full knowledge of each section sub-vocally.*

She gave the voice credit on one account. It wasn't exactly glib. It told her what it wanted and she gave it and that was that, no further discussion. If she didn't give it, a brief reminder of Zernin-deprivation shot through her.

She assumed that it was storing up this information for Zarpfrin. The bastard hadn't told her that the device he'd planted this time had a brain of its own, though it made sense.

The thing functioned as a kind of conscience for her. She had the distinct feeling that Arnal Zarpfrin was peering over her shoulder, chuckling softly to himself about his ingenuity. The irony of the situation was that it was so much like the last time: if she didn't have so much other paraphernalia riding around inside her, this implant would be detected immediately by any cursory *Starbow* sensor check. The last time, though, she wasn't aware of an implant's existence. This time she was aware —but she could do nothing about it.

They had just passed through the hydroponics section and approached a door with an off-limits insignia.

Enter this door.

Sorry, Laura thought silently, communicating to the voice. Strictly off-limits. There's a lot on board the ship that I'm not going to be able to get into. And if I do, they'll suspect me and detain me and find out maybe that I'm about three ounces heavier than before I made the trip down to Walthor."

Understood. Should opportunity arise, take it.

Very well, you bastard. But I won't like it.

Please desist with rebellious attitude. Warning. Warning!

Humorless shit! Even talking with Zarpfrin was better than this! She wanted to collapse and cry, but feared that the implant would interpret this as a threat and deal with it accordingly.

"Pilot Laura Shemzak!" an announcement blared over a loudspeaker. "Please report to Captain's cabin."

What could they want from her now? Couldn't they just let her wander around in peace for a while, before she had to gallivant off on another mission?

She dragged toward the lift.

Attitude uncharacteristic, said the voice. *Please assume normal manner lest suspicion fall.*

"Goddammit! Fragging demands! Demands! Demands!" she yelped. She formed a fist and hit a bulkhead.

Excellent.

She had to laugh.

"So what the hell do you want now, Northern?"

Laura Shemzak paraded into the room and plopped down on a chair, lifting her boots onto a table. Despite everything that had happened, despite the despair that lingered deep within her, she didn't feel too bad.

Maybe the goddamned implant had increased her Zernin supply or something. Whatever it was, she was finally beginning to feel fit and feisty again.

Captain Northern was stone-cold sober, drinking soda water flavored with some exotic citrus fruit.

"I want to go over some things with you," he said in a businesslike tone. Then he broke out in a smile. "By the way, Laura, you're looking quite beautiful. A day's rest has been good for you."

"Yeah, and a bath and a change of clothing." The ship's store had asked her what kind of clothes she wanted. She refused the standard *Starbow* uniform in favor of duplicates of her favored night-black jumpsuit and glossy boots, offset with a bright red scarf. "You don't look so bad yourself."

He looked crisp, clean, and efficient in his casual khakis, complete with epaulets and brass buttons.

"Another adventure. But more to come, I think, for you and I?" His eyes glimmered strangely.

Watch out! she thought. And he hadn't even been drinking!

From the beginning he'd been attracted to her. The astonishing thing was that lately she realized that she wasn't just infatuated with this handsome, erratic, but very personable starship captain. She had deeper feelings for him. Feelings that had grown as she had learned about the man's faults and the deeper things about him: his loyalty to his friends, his allegiance to his cause, his love for his ideals. All beneath his exasperatingly playful and cynical veneer.

That he was terminally sexy with his beautiful eyes and chiseled features and wild rumpled hair, didn't help much.

And here he was, getting interested in her too! Laura Shemzak the walking booby trap; the druggie who in her very return to the *Starbow* had betrayed its crew, its cause . . . and a man she cared for—its captain.

It took her just a twinkling of a moment to realize what she had to do.

"We've been through a lot, Northern," she said caustically. "And we've got a lot more to go through before this wretched business is all through. Let's keep the flirtation to an absolute minimum, okay?"

His mouth twitched, his eyes blinked, and for a second she saw a spark of hurt in them. Then he looked away.

"Yes. Yes, you're absolutely correct, Pilot." When he looked back again, his expression was cut from stone. "Actually, there were other things that we have to discuss. For that reason I have taken the liberty of calling Chivon Lasster up here. She should be here soon. In the meantime, can I get you something to drink?"

"Yeah. How about some of that stuff you got from your pal on Kendrick's Vision. Brandy is it?"

A bemused expression came to Northern's face.

"Laura, I thought you said that you didn't drink because it was bad for your nervous system as a blip-ship pilot!"

"This whole goddamn trip has been bad for my nervous system!" she almost shouted. "A couple swigs of brandy ain't gonna do it that much more harm." She shrugged, quieting. "Besides, Dansen Jitt tells me that there's no way we're going to make it back to Earth from here in less than a week."

"Right, and during which time we're going to have to figure out how to get through the considerable Solar System defenses unnoticed. But that's neither here nor there, Laura. You still are just not a drinker. You know, even with all the medical backup systems in this day and age, the junk really isn't good for you."

"You're worried about what's good for me when I'm about to be sent off on another suicide mission?" She chuckled. "Just shut up and pour me the stuff."

Northern went to his cabinet, pulled out a bottle and a glass, and poured.

"More," she said.

Northern shrugged and poured the glass three-quarters full. He gave it to Laura, who stared at it a moment, then sipped it tentatively.

Her first impulse was to spit it out, but she managed to get it down without too much grimacing, and after a moment of disconcern in her stomach area, a warmth spread.

"I can feel it eating away at my stomach lining," she said. She began to feel a little dizzy. "Now it's after the brain cells."

"I told you, my dear. Perhaps you should give me that glass back."

"Hell, no!" She took another sip, larger this time. This went down a little easier. "I can handle it. I'm gonna need something if I gotta talk to that Lasster bitch." The sensation from the drink seemed to loosen her tongue, and she looked at Northern in a sarcastic, squinty way. "I guess now that she's come over to your side, you two can get back together again, eh?"

Northern raised his eyebrows. "I think that despite our past, at this point that's highly unlikely, Laura." He smiled lightly. "What's wrong. Jealous?"

Warning, said the voice within her. *Depart from this line of conversation.*

"Jealous of that chunk of ice?" Laura responded immediately. "You've gotta be kidding. Let's just drop this, okay, and get on toward important stuff like saving those Whositwhatsis pals of Mish, so we can finally get on with getting my brother out of the fix he's in. That is the main reason I'm here, you know."

Commendable, said the voice.

"It all ties in together," said Northern nonchalantly.

"Unless we get blown up by the Federation!" Laura burst out. "With Lasster's defection, you can bet that old Zarpfrin is gonna double-team efforts to nail our asses!"

Of course, her own tail still smarted from the puncture wound.

"I am well aware of the situation, Laura," said Northern. "But Zarpfrin is surely not planning on a visit to Terra from the *Starbow*.

Yeah, but he would find out soon enough.

Curiously, the alcohol seemed to dim her desire to confess the whole thing to the man, and maybe save the *Starbow*. Right now, she just didn't give a damn.

Exemplary! commented the voice. It sounded a little strange, but Laura hardly noticed, since it seemed to let a little more Zernin into her blood system.

She was starting to really fly now—she felt great, and she really didn't care much about anything else but feeling great.

There was a knock at the door. Northern punched a button, allowing entrance to Chivon Lasster.

She walked in coolly and sat down with a polite nod to Laura. The urge to thumb her nose at Chivon was strong, but Laura contained it.

Chivon wore a more informal version of the khakis that Northern wore, and Laura was sorry to see that she looked good in them. Her hair was much the same as Laura remembered from their last encounter on Earth: blond, with bangs. Her no-nonsense nose and faintly pointed chin were both turned up slightly too high for Laura's taste.

Still, she had bailed Northern out of trouble—and apparently, judging from Zarpfrin's reaction, she was on the up and up. No goddamn voices ringing in *her* head.

"Thank you for coming, Chivon."

"I am, of course, at your service, Captain Northern."

"I just *bet* you are," sniped Laura, gripping her glass tightly.

Chivon glanced over to the blip-ship pilot and said, "I thought you didn't drink, Laura. Clearly, you shouldn't."

"I can do what I goddamn well please," returned Laura. "I've been here longer than you."

"I don't believe that either of you are ranked aboard the *Starbow*," said Northern. "And I'm not about to play favorites. Believe it or not, I actually want to hash out something serious here that only the three of us can really talk about."

"And what's that?" asked Laura.

"Arnal Zarpfrin. Our dear Friend. Machiavelli of the starways."

"He's a Feddy," said Laura, eyeing Chivon distastefully. "He's a baddie. That's his job."

"No, I've been putting this and that together. The lack of Jaxdron activity on Walthor indicates that if there is indeed a spy operation being conducted within the human-held worlds, it's controlled by the Federation. Which makes one ask, how did the Jaxdron find out about the project on Mulliphen, and specifically, how did they find out about the abilities of Calspar Shemzak?"

"I wish I could tell you," said Chivon softly. "But that wasn't my area of management."

"Another factor, then. This business on Kendrick's Vision. The Jaxdron had Freeman Jonst scared so shitless, he was willing to seek protection from the Federation."

"That's becoming a common occurrence these days," said Chivon. "It's a fairly obvious situation. We have a war going with a powerful civilization and the Federation has been using that war to renegotiate ties with the Free Worlds in return for protection."

"But, of course, once they get enough ships for protection around these planets, they can just take them over again!"

"That is a possibility that Zarpfrin mentioned, and I was fully aware of that, as were all Friends. We all desired the return of as many Free Worlds as possible to the Federation fold, in the least violent manner."

"Hmm. And I bet that dear old Zarpy has been making a lot of trips lately, hasn't he?"

"Well, yes, he has, as far as I can tell."

"This whole way he dealt with you, Laura," said Northern. "Mish and I have run an analysis on it, and it indeed fits a predictable pattern. Now, let's hypothesize upon a few facts, shall we? For a bunch of nasty, awful, powerful, planet-hungry bug-eyed monsters, the Jaxdron have certainly done a minimum amount of damage. Oh, sure, they've taken a few worlds, but the Federation and the Free Worlds constitute thousands of planets. And sure, there have been some space battles between fleets, but not really that many. It's my opinion, and Mish's, that all of this has been for show."

"Just a goddamned minute!" Laura said. "We know the Jaxdron exist. We've fought with them. And their ships sure weren't built by the Federation. Jitt got that psychic message and—"

Northern held up a hand. "Whoa there, lady. Hold your horses. How's that for an expression you might use?" He smiled. "I'm not saying the Jaxdron don't exist. I'm just saying that they're not really interested in taking over the human-held worlds that much. What I'm saying is that, in fact, Arnal Zarpfrin contacted them sometime back and made some unholy alliance, some complex deal with them. Complex, of course, because it fully plays into what the Jaxdron want . . . which, of course, is the X factor. All we know is that they want to use Cal Shemzak—and they want the secret that's aboard this ship. But then everyone does. No, there *is* more, but we have to discover that from them and them alone."

Chivon was astonished. "Yes . . . Yes, that would make sense. But if that is what Zarpfrin has been doing, then it's without the full knowledge of the Council."

"Which is possible?"

"I've learned in the past weeks, Northern, that anything is possible."

"Right. So it seems simple enough, once you've got past the idea of Zarpfrin getting through to the Jaxdron, communicating with them, and striking some sort of a deal. The Jaxdron play the bogeyman, scare the daylights out of the Free Worlds, and one by one they seek help from Big Daddy Federation. Planet after planet will be inducted back into the Federation, whether they like it or not. Guys like Freeman Jonst will wake up one morning with a skyfull of Feddy ships and the message, "You're part of the gang again!"

"But why would Zarpfrin allow the Jaxdron to destroy the project and take Cal?" asked Laura, playing along.

"Simple. Zarpfrin is really against any kind of project that will open up more space. It's like I mentioned before—why he's frightened of the portals. He doesn't want to go any farther. There are more powerful civilizations out there in the Universe. He wants mankind to develop in different ways, to perhaps become more advanced and powerful and militaristic in order to prepare to spread out farther and not get conquered. But he also wants to consolidate the human-held worlds already in existence. And along the way, wipe out gadflies like us starhounds on the *Starbow*."

Chivon nodded. "Yes. Yes, that must be it!"

"So Laura, there are still unanswered questions in why he allowed you to go out to try to rescue Cal. Part of it has to do certainly with the possibility of your running into us, which he saw on his computers. But there's more. More that can only be discovered by finding out fully what the Jaxdron want."

"But we're still going after Cal, then," said Laura.

"Oh, definitely," said Northern. "I just wanted to puzzle some things out, see if there's anything you two can add."

Plenty, thought Laura, if only I could.

"Nothing," said Chivon. "Only from everything that Zarpfrin has said to me—and the things he hasn't said—

this sounds like an excellent explanation.''

"Sounds like he wants more than just the good of the Federation to me,'' said Laura.

"Yes,'' said Northern. "That's highly likely.''

"The ultimate dream of a megalomaniac,'' said Chivon. "And power beyond the imagination. . . .''

"Yes,'' said Northern. "I do believe that old Zarpy wants quite a bit more than he lets on.''

Chapter Seven

Chivon Lasster knew the *Starbow* from her days as its copilot. Nonetheless, she was astonished at the variety of changes effected upon the ship in these past years. They were three days short of Earth, the crew relaxing after their feverish adventures, and for the first time in years, Chivon felt truly rested—rested and safe. She and Northern had agreed that her role would be minimal for a time—best for her mental health—and she would be called upon only if truly needed.

Which was fine by her, since life aboard the *Starbow* was so strange to her now.

One of the robots—named Alexander the Great—was delegated as her guide and servant, and, she suspected, her keeper. She elected to tour the areas of the *Starbow* to which she was allowed access.

The others of the crew remained friendly but slightly aloof. She couldn't blame them. After all, here in their midst was a person who had once sworn to capture them. A hated Friend of the Federation. It would take more than a while for them to warm up to someone like herself—especially since Chivon's personality was not exactly congenial and warm, as she well knew. Still, that was all right, since she needed time to herself to think things out.

The one individual she missed the most was Andrew. He was the one person she felt she could really trust, who seemed to know her better than she knew herself. She could talk to Andrew, really talk. About anything. She missed that. A fleeting thought came to her that since Dr. Mish was the same sort of being as Andrew, that perhaps she might be able to talk to him. . . .

But, of course, that was impossible. One of the reasons that Andrew had been so good with her was that he was a CompComp—an official Computer Companion with total access to all the records the Federation kept on each individual from birth. Andrew knew her favorite colors, what her aptitude was for card games, how many lovers she had had—*everything*. To this, of course, he had added his special brand of ancient wisdom—alien wisdom at that, she thought wryly—which surely Mish had too. But there was no way she could ever begin to give Mish all the information that Andrew had.

Perhaps it was just as well, she thought. She had to learn to depend upon herself for these kinds of things—especially since, for the sake of unselfish principles totally new to her, she had just ripped herself away from the social structure from which her mind had literally grown.

Yes, she thought as she idly browsed through the ship's library, Alexander quietly waiting in a chair, it was best to make these kinds of adjustments on her own.

When Andrew had first revealed to her his true identity, along with the fact that four others like him hid within the electronic nooks and crannies of Federation computers, Chivon's paranoia was set off. She had always secretly feared that Andrew was a ploy on the part of other competitive Friends after her job. Or even that the Council was checking on her loyalty.

But Andrew's story rang true. It made sense.

This was why Arnal Zarpfrin had destroyed the sentient ships, not because they were artificially intelligent, but because they were alien ships, each holding portals to who-knows-where. By destroying them, he thought he would eradicate the threat to humanity from the many nameless civilizations Out There.

Also, the creature she dealt with, this Aspach, as it called itself and its fellows, was simply too coherently *good* to be the product of Federation minds. He had an almost discernible integrity that radiated from his presence. Alas, Andrew could tell her very little of his past. Like Dr. Mish, he and his fellow Aspach had lost much of their memory—there seemed to be some mosaic, some puzzle involved in their existence that would only be solved by a reuniting of their full number with one of the portals they inhabited.

This was why Andrew had ventured out to seek assistance from Chivon. Only with her help could the *Starbow* be called back and contact be made.

She only thought about it for a very short time before she had decided that she would indeed defect from the Federation, abandoning her home and her career. All her ambition, encouraged by the Federation, had never led her to anything truly satisfying.

She had been content only one time in her life—when she had been with Tars Northern. For years after he fled Earth, she had tried to deny this fact, which was why she had needed the therapeutic assistance of a Comp-Comp in the first place.

Perhaps, she thought, now that she realized why Tars had abandoned her, in her heart of hearts she forgave him. He had stolen the *Starbow* to save it, after all, and in so doing had become an outlaw in the eyes of the Federation. He had sacrificed all for the sake of his newly formed ideals, and for the sake of his rebellion against the restrictive tyrannical reign of the Federation over the human spirit—over human freedom. And once that was thoroughly understood in her own mind, she realized that he had done the right thing, and that she should do the right thing as well.

This, Andrew told her, was the possibility that he had seen in her psychological profile: the potential for renewal, the capacity for idealism. What he hadn't added was *potential for salvation*, though Chivon knew that now to be true.

She had done the right thing, and now she had to

figure out what that meant in her life.

Being around Tars Northern again was strange as well, and something that she had to adjust to slowly: the man had changed.

The fact that she was confused about how she felt about him now might indeed have been complicating her perceptions. When she had been with him before, Tars had been of rock-solid character, a hero with a sense of humor but a troubled mind. He had been a most competent captain and pilot who took great pleasure in his position. He loved his ships, he loved his job. They had met before being assigned as copilots to the *Starbow*, but did not become lovers until they were placed together on the vessel. The changes had started when he met Dr. Mish, and now, years later, they seemed complete.

Oh, Tars Northern still had his integrity—but the spontaneous nature of the man had come out, the unpredictability. Certainly he was still talented and competent; but now there was an excitement to his eyes as though at times he dwelled totally only in the present moment.

Yes, and there was more mystery now. . . .

She tried to avoid him as much as possible.

She had admitted to Andrew that she still loved the man. A difficult confession, because the Federation enculturation always instilled the notion in its citizens that romantic love did not exist. Seeing him now, different yet more exciting, made her want him more.

She needed to control that. She needed to get herself together, under tight rein again, especially since she didn't have Andrew for therapy.

Control. Aloofness. Those were the things that Chi von Lasster sought now, and she appreciated the *Starbow* crew for their willingness to give her the space she needed.

Perhaps she could get to know them better later; and then she would open herself more to them.

She was in the library with Alexander, absently considering this, when the woman introduced to her before as Midshipman Gemma Naquist entered the room.

"Oh, hello," said the midshipman. "I hope I'm not intruding. Just thought I'd check out a book spool."

"Intruding?" Chivon immediately realized that this was a perfect example of what she'd been considering. "No, of course not. If anything, perhaps I am the intruder."

"That why you've been keeping to yourself?" the spunky, friendly-eyed woman wanted to know, clearly giving Chivon a chance to confide in her. "We're quite grateful about the way you snatched our dear captain from the hands of the enemy."

"It was something I thought necessary." There was a moment of awkwardness. She paused for a moment, then smiled. "I am sorry, but you must realize that I feel myself in a peculiar situation."

"Oh . . . you being a Friend and all that." Gemma nodded. "Well, you have to remember that all of us have peculiar backgrounds—or why would we be aboard the *Starbow*?"

Gemma browsed through a catalog, checking titles. She seemed a bright, energetic person, and quite attractive in a personable way. Perhaps here was the opportunity to try to get to know at least one of the crew better.

"I guess, then, you know my background," she said coolly.

"Sure," replied Gemma jauntily. "You used to hold a top position in Feddy bureaucracy." She turned a sly smile on her. "And a little bird told me you used to be the captain's lady."

Chivon found herself laughing at the frankness of that last remark. "Yes, I suppose you could say that."

"Must have been tough. That Northern can be rough on women. Glad I never got involved with him." She said it so casually that Chivon suddenly found she could at last discuss that most complex man, Tars Northern.

"Yes. I interviewed a lady named Kat Mizel who seemed rather perturbed over the subject."

Gemma laughed. "And damned perturbed she got left behind in that raid, I don't doubt. Poor Kat's only problem was that she had it pretty bad for the captain. So bad, in fact, she tricked the guy into marrying her when he was loaded and on a shore leave."

"Ah," said Chivon. So that was why Tars Northern got married. His drinking and his integrity . . . a curious combination.

"So what happened to old Kat, anyway." Gemma put a hand to her hip and flashed a frown at Chivon. "The way we figure, she helped old Zarpfrin . . . and you . . . get tabs on us. Helped you lay that trap on—."

"Zarpfrin sent her to a rehabilitation planet somewhere. In a few more months, I daresay she'll be a good Federation citizen."

"Nothing much more she can do against us, I suppose. Still, it is a shame the way things turned out. Maybe we'll run into Kat again, somewhere down the line. I hope so."

"I don't think she'd very much like to see me again," said Chivon.

"No, I suppose she wouldn't."

"Laura Shemzak has a bit of a . . . what would you call it . . . a crush? An affection for Tars. Something she tries to hide."

"You've noticed so soon. Oh, yes, and I think there's something for her in him. . . ."

"Oh?"

"Yeah, like raw lust."

Chivon stifled a snort.

"Yes, half the women that have been on this boat have developed a thing for good Captain Northern," Gemma said. "I suppose it's the romantic dash in the man. I confess, sometimes it gets to me too."

"I think he enjoys that. But tell me, Gemma . . . you

said you had an unusual induction aboard the *Starbow*. I'd like to hear about it.''

"We all had unusual inductions . . . and adjustments. Northern plied the oddball corners of the Free Worlds, where the flotsam and jetsam of humanity gravitate—"

"To hang out in bars?''

"I think he wanted to recruit people who were experienced and talented . . . but disillusioned, and perhaps desperate. Desperate enough to join this crew, anyway. Oh, and one more characteristic is needed.''

"Oh? And what's that?'' Chivon asked.

"A certain idealism. I think that at the core of every member of this crew is a belief in the value of the individual's freedom. The belief that human beings have the right to shape their own destinies, not be controlled by some greater, mindless set of cultural attitudes. Know what I mean?''

"Oh, yes,'' Chivon replied. "That's ninety percent of how the Federation controls its citizens, the other ten percent being the genetic programming, the intensely controlled education, the monitored competition and achievement—"

"Oh, yeah,'' Gemma interrupted. "We all heard about that on Anteres IV.''

"Anteres IV, that's the Free World you're from?''

"Uh-huh.''

A beautiful, very docile world as I recall,'' Chivon said. "Blue skies. Lots of grass and water and farming and dairy operations. Manufactures the best cheese in the galaxy.''

"Hey, you know your planets, don't you?''

"I had to. Part of my job was to study methods for infiltration and takeover of a large sector of Free Worlds through nonviolent means.''

"Yeah, well, they can have Anteres IV, far as I'm concerned,'' Gemma said. "Boring as they come.''

"That's why you joined up with the *Starbow*? You did promise to tell me about it.'' It was then that Chivon noticed the freckles that dusted the midshipman's nose and cheeks, or at least they seemed more pronounced. And the former Friend could visualize this affable, open human being wandering in the pastures beneath a pair of rosy suns, a stereotypical corn-fed girl.

"Oh, yes. I joined planet's National Guard first, against the wishes of my parents. They wanted me to marry some clodhopper and cut sod and feed cows and squeeze out a load of healthy babies. I learned to fly the third-rate airboats and system ships, but there were no real challenges. So one day, while stationed in the capital, I'm looking over the classifieds in the local rag because there wasn't anything much better to do, and I come across this ad. Let me see if I can remember the exact wording: WANTED. SOLDIER OF FORTUNE. MILITARY AND SPACE PILOTING EXPERIENCE DESIRABLE. PREFERABLY ATTRACTIVE FEMALE. And the recruitment place was this local dive. So I thought, Hey, why not? See what this joker is up to. I mean, I'm not bad looking and I did fit the bill."

"So you went to the bar and got in line."

"Line? No way. I was the only one who showed up. So Northern is sitting at this dark corner table. I know this is the guy because Arkm Thur came up to the bar where I'm sitting with my beer and he taps me on the arm and asks me if I'm here about the ad. So I say maybe, and he smiles and says 'Good enough,' and takes me back to Northern.

"So here's this crazy ex-Feddy pilot and we get along great. I drink a little too much . . . well, a lot too much, and they tell me they'd really like me aboard the *Starbow*. They tell me how exciting it is, what great adventures, what great people . . . you know, the whole recruitment thing. I said, I'd have to desert the Anteres National Guard, and Northern says, 'No problem. I've got a friend high up in the military here. We can make arrangements.' So the next thing I know, I've got myself packed and I'm sipping a beer on one of the *Starbow*'s shuttles . . .

"And let me guess the rest. The Anteres Navy started chasing you," said Chivon.

"No! After I woke up the next morning I was sure that I was shanghaied, and I made all kinds of fuss. But then Northern played back this taped transmission, and damned if it wasn't a general in the Anteres Defense Force, friendly as you please with the guy, giving me the full go ahead! Northern even let me send back a message to say good-bye and see you later to my relatives. I mean, he's nasty sometimes, but he's really a pretty good guy on the whole. The way I figure it, I never did really desert my National Guard. I'm kind of doing my job here, instead. And it's an important job." She glanced at the file in front of Chivon and said, "Hey, you want to have a cup of coffee or something?"

For a moment something in Chivon held back, but it was just an automatic reflex and she saw it as such.

"Sure," she said. "Why not?"

On the way to the mess, Gemma said, "Some ship, huh?"

"Oh, yes indeed. Some ship."

"Oh, right. I forgot. You know it pretty well already . . . you used to be the copilot."

"Well, I didn't know that it held a plugged-up portal to some different dimension, I can tell you that. That's certainly new to me. And this alien . . . What's his name?"

"Shontill."

"Yes, the one in search of his lost race. He's new to me as well. An interesting being, Shontill. He seemed very disturbed at the delay. Though I must say, he is a fascinating creature."

"Say, how about a little field trip?" said Gemma.

"Pardon?"

"We're talking about Shontill . . . why don't we talk

to him? Yes. It would help you get a better idea of what the *Starbow* is about.''

''Are you sure that's good idea?''

Gemma grinned. ''Sure I am. I get along with Shontill okay. I guess you've never spoken much to aliens, eh?''

''Not in any depth.''

''Shontill's okay . . . and you know, the more aliens I meet—and we've met a few, believe me—the more I realize that humans have more in common with other intelligences than they realize. I mean, we all *exist*, don't we, and we've got to deal with being alive and aware . . . Sure, the details are different, but at the core, we're all in the same boat.''

''An interesting philosophical position,'' Chivon said dryly.

A spark of fire ignited in Gemma's clear eyes. ''You don't believe me, do you?'' She grinned maliciously. ''Oh yeah, I remember. Your brains were parboiled by the Federation.''

Chivon blinked and stepped back as though struck in the face. Then she laughed when she realized that there was a joke behind the sting. ''Perhaps. Very well, then, Midshipman Naquist. Lead me to this Shontill creature and I will speak to him, if you insist.''

''Sure, it'll do you good,'' Gemma said brightly. ''Expand your mind and all that.''

''Shall we ask him to join us?''

''Oh, no, that's okay. I was going down to say hello sometime soon anyway. Shontill's been keeping to his quarters lately. I think he's depressed. Maybe we'll cheer him up. Come on. It's on the next level down.''

They found the lift and descended.

''Don't you need permission from the captain or something?''

''No, I've got access.'' Gemma lifted her hand, showing her palm. ''Programmed into my identipad here.''

The door they stopped in front of had a jamb limned in black and yellow striping. Gemma stopped for a mo-

ment in front of it, examining her imprint, tapping it
into action with a forefinger. She pressed it on the side
of the door and the door clicked.

It began to slide open.

Chivon was immediately aware of the different smell,
and then the different temperature of the room.

"Breathable, but not pleasant," she said as a gust of
it poured out.

"You'll get used to it," Gemma remarked blithely as
the door finished opening. "Bit of sulfur, rotten egg
stuff . . . but actually the mix is good for your sinuses,
believe it or not."

"Warmer," said Chivon. "Shontill comes from a
tropical climate?"

"Apparently . . . at least that's the condition he's
most comfortable in. Of course, he's quite able to roam
about in our standard atmosphere with the proper adjustments. A pretty remarkable fellow, Shontill. Highly
adaptable."

They stepped through the door.

"It's like a jungle in here," said Chivon, noticing in
the dim lighting the fronds and vines and flowers draped
from the ceiling.

"Yeah, nice isn't it? Dr. Mish fixed this up after we
discovered Shontill in the wreckage of that starship . . .
even before we could speak with the guy. Mish just took
a scan of the unconscious alien's biological makeup,
made certain deductions, and voilà! A home for our
guest."

Chivon looked around, shivering a bit despite herself.

"Hey, Shontill!" called Gemma. "You've got company in your waiting room. It's me, Midshipman
Gemma, and a friend. Are you decent?"

There was no response. Only the sounds of distant
fluid gurgling.

"Hmm," said Gemma. "He must be snoozing in his
rest chamber."

"Well, then, we don't want to wake him up, do we?"

Chivon said tightly, feeling ill at ease.

"Oh, don't worry. I've gotten him out of sleep before. It's really quite a sight, anyway, dear Shontill in his watery form. We should at least have a peek."

Gemma grabbed her by the arm and lightly tugged her along. "Oh, c'mon. You've opted for a life of adventure by hopping on this tug. Let's start right now."

A faint phosphorescence glowed on the walls of the next room. A bit of wet vegetation slapped Chivon in the face as she passed through an oval portal behind Gemma.

One entire wall seemed to be a tank of some kind, in which strands of something floated.

Gemma seemed concerned. "Something's not right," she said.

"What do you mean?" Chivon asked.

"Well . . . that's where he should be," Gemma replied, pointing at the empty tank.

Chivon took a backward step. "Maybe he went to the toilet. We really shouldn't—"

"He *could* be out talking with Mish, though it seems—"

That was when the creature attacked.

It swooped out of a corner, bellowing—a horrible, bloated parody of the alien that Chivon had seen before, its eyes red and huge and glittering in the low light.

"Shontill!" Gemma cried, startled. "What's—"

Her sentence changed to a yelp as Shontill's tentacle whipped around and struck her, sending Gemma thudding against the wall.

Chivon leaped back, fighting panic.

Something was definitely wrong here, but what could she do?

The answer came to her immediately: *Get out of here!*

The alien was making a terrible shrieking noise, as though in pain. Or was that its language?

Gemma was a heap on the floor, attempting to stand up. Shontill seemed to be undergoing contortions, as though fighting its raging condition.

"Nooooo," it croaked. *"Noooooooo!"*

Seeing the alien's condition, Chivon restrained her urge to flee. She grabbed Gemma from behind and hauled her up, dragging her back toward the entrance. They had made it halfway when, with a roar, Shontill started to follow in a loping crawl.

"Gemma, come on, you've got to help!" grunted Chivon.

Gemma managed to get her feet under her, though she didn't seem to know which way to go. Leading her, Chivon urged, "Hurry! Hurry!"

The mindless rage overcame the alien again. It was a big thing, and it banged against the side of the portal as it emerged into the brighter light. Its gray-green hide was now a rainbow of slick running stuff from open sores. Drool splashed from an open mouth holding sharp and ragged teeth. Its alien eyes started from its head, and its veined nostrils flared.

They got to the door. Chivon pushed Gemma through.

Just as she was about to step through herself, something grabbed hold of her wrist and spun her about. She found herself inches from Shontill's horrible countenance. Using reserves she hadn't tapped in years, she flung herself back, pulling a tentacle along with her.

"Close the door!" she screamed.

Gemma, still dim-eyed, but active now, was already at the side of the door, palm against the code sequencer.

Click.

The door rolled closed quickly, crashing against the ropy tentacle, wedging it in the opening.

The alien howled with pain, and the limb lost its grasp on Chivon's arm.

"Communicator at end of the hall!" Gemma cried

weakly. Chivon saw twin streams of blood running down her cheeks from her scalp. "Security. Emergency in section ten. Hurry!"

The tentacle writhed and whipped about as Shontill madly pounded against the partially open door.

After a breathless race down the hall, Chivon found the communicator and called for security.

The robots were there within one minute.

Shontill's tentacle had transformed into something more handlike, but it was still stuck in the door. Greenish blood was oozing along the doorjamb. The door bowed under the powerful creature's blows. Its howls had become terrifying shrieks.

"Right!" said General Montgomery. "What's the trouble?"

"Can't you see?" Chivon cried, pointing at the mess. "That alien has gone berserk!"

There were two other robots, and two more were running down the hall toward them, holding stun guns. The robot called Montgomery assayed the situation quickly, then stepped over to the wall beside the door. "Prepare weapons!" he ordered. "Midshipman Naquist, if you would open the door."

"Don't hurt him," Naquist demanded, wiping the blood from her eyes.

"Some hurt will be necessary, I think. We just won't kill him," responded the robot.

"Good enough," said the midshipman, immediately coding open the door.

Shontill stumbled out, enraged, and immediately met with a net of crisscrossing beams.

The alien charged on, swiping one of his assailants against the side of the head, sending it crashing into pieces against the wall.

The alien turned as the stun beams continued to hit it, finally causing it to tumble unconscious to the floor.

"I think," said Gemma, "we'd better get Dr. Mish down here."

Chapter Eight

Calling Dr. Michael Mish was not necessary. He arrived soon after the maddened alien had been stunned into submission.

The white-haired Mish shook his head and clucked over the sprawled body. "Oh, dear, I have been much too preoccupied," he said, making a cursory scan with his sensor board. "I really should have seen this coming."

"Hey, what about me? I'm kind of smashed up too!" Gemma said, clearly annoyed.

"Come along to my lab and we'll give you a patch-up as well," said Mish. He turned to the robots. "Now, gentlemen, if you would be so kind as to go back and fetch a gurney to help me carry this heavy beast back . . ."

Chivon shook her head clear of the heavy mist of shock that seemed to fill it. "What could have happened?"

"We forgot to take into account, I suspect, the differences of psychological patterns in Shontill. He always has been, after all, quite despondent because of his need to find his lost race. Perhaps his physiological transitions were somehow disrupted when he came so close when we found that Frin'ral wreck. And now he's had to wait longer. And also, perhaps he didn't tell us some things about his nature. I should have monitored him more closely, but I have been so busy. . . ."

The alien made a moaning sound and trembled slightly. Gills to the side of his neck flapped out and were sucked in.

"Looks like you caught him in the midst of some kind

of transformation. What were you doing down there, anyway?"

"Just stopped in to visit," Gemma said defensively. "I thought it would be a good idea if Chivon had a word or two with the big guy."

"It's just as well," came a voice from behind them. "No one was hurt seriously, and now we can do something for Shontill."

Chivon turned and saw Captain Northern approaching them.

"I've been watching," he said by way of explanation. "Couldn't get down here immediately, so I turned on the monitors. Are you two all right?"

"It was rather frightening," Chivon said in a monotone, fighting the urge to fling herself into his arms.

The robots returned with the gurney.

"Take good care of him," Northern said as the robots hauled the alien up atop the cart.

"Him?" said Gemma. "What about me?"

"I told you, I'd take care of you," said Dr. Mish, peering up from his ministrations to Shontill. "Sick bay is after all adjacent to my lab."

"You can be part of Mish's infamous experiments," Northern said brightly.

"Just looking for attention," Gemma said.

"We'll check around later," said Northern. "I really want to know what caused this." He turned to Chivon. "Let's go get something for those nerves. I assume you still favor sparkle-whiskey."

Chivon nodded.

"I happen to have a very nice brand I've been saving just for you. Let's go have a drop."

"I really shouldn't. I don't have my biomonitoring devices here."

"What do you think I use? You'll be okay. A small glass won't hurt."

"I'm just worried about damage . . . and addiction, I guess."

"Darling, as a new and possibly permanent passenger aboard the *Starbow*, I should tell you that there are a lot greater dangers than alcohol in store for you here."

Later in the day Dr. Mish alerted the captain that Shontill had pulled through his biological troubles, was fully conscious, and was ready to speak.

Because the rest of the crew was concerned about the alien, Northern authorized that certain of the higher-ranked members be present.

Laura Shemzak did not particularly care to be there.

But her voice demanded that she go.

Actually, she was shocked that Northern believed her story about her concern for the well-being of the alien. She did not get along well with Shontill. However, she had reminded him of her interest in getting into Omega Space—a matter in which Shontill played an important part. Therefore, she was concerned about everything that happened to the creature.

Apparently, Northern was preoccupied enough to accept the reason, she thought—most likely because of the drinks he'd been having with that bitch Chivon Lasster.

Poor Shontill was strapped inside a colloidal tank by tubing and wires. Bubbles gently coursed up his hide. His huge eyes were only half open, but fairly alert. Certainly they had none of the madness that Lasster and Naquist had seen; only a resigned sadness that touched something deep in Laura.

Boy, I know how you feel, buddy, she thought. What a rotten universe!

"How's he doing, Doctor?" asked Northern as the others formed an uncomfortable group, keeping their distance from the imprisoned alien.

"Life signs back to acceptability and exhibiting general docility, Captain."

"Any idea about what set him off?" asked Arkm Thur.

"A combination of two things, apparently. First, our guest is going through some sort of metabolic and structural change, which seems in keeping with his genetic code. A Frin'ral rite of passage, it seems, that could be aided by the presence of others of his race. I haven't quite figured it out yet, but it's not necessarily sexual, although it could have something to do with Frin'ral bonding patterns.

"The second reason has more to do with us. Apparently, Shontill is having the Frin'ral equivalent of a nervous breakdown. He is despondent about our lack of action, our detours from the attempt to find his people."

"But doesn't he understand that it's all a part of the master plan?" asked Gemma Naquist.

Her head was bandaged, which was unnecessary, Laura thought, since any wounds could easily be covered by dermaplast: Gemma probably wore the bandage to be dramatic, Laura decided, knowing she would have done the same thing.

"Apparently, his change is fouling up his reasoning ability."

Shontill opened his mouth and uttered a few alien words that sounded like a broken garbage converter.

"I say he's in heat or something," Laura said.

"You have him under sedation?" asked the captain.

"The safest I can devise for his chemical makeup," returned Mish.

Northern stepped forward, closer to the beast. "Shontill, this is Captain Northern. Can you hear me?"

The eyes turned Northern's way, brighter.

"That's right. The chap that saved your ass. Is there anything we can do, Shontill?"

This time the alien managed to speak in their language. "We must . . . find my . . . people soon." The eyes seemed infinitely sad. "Soon . . . or you must . . . destroy me!"

"Shontill, if you could explain what's happening

to you, I might be able to help," said Mish, clearly alarmed.

"The Time . . . it is the Time of the Turn. . . . I have dreaded this. The Time . . ."

"What's he saying?" said Gemma. "Something about the Time? But what does that mean, Shontill? Truly, we want to help!"

Suddenly, the alien's pupils dilated.

The beepers on Mish's machinery began to scream insistently.

His body began to shiver violently. His powerful limbs strained against the lashings that held him.

"He's going nuts again, Doctor," said Gemma, flinching away, the memory of the alien's previous violence clearly playing across her features. "Do something."

"The miniature tractor beams," Northern said, pointing toward a collection of equipment in the corner. "Hurry."

Several attendant robots snapped to duty, scurrying over toward the machines Northern indicated.

But Laura could see that it would be too late—much too late. Already the restraints were snapping—the nutrient fluid splashed over the top of the tank from the creature's frenetic activity.

"Stand back!" someone yelled, but Laura had already hustled back a few strides into safety, unable to keep her eyes off of Shontill and his mad efforts to break his bonds.

The thick-muscled tentacles broke free and burst up into the air, splattering fluid against the wall. They came down hard on the rim of the tank, breaking the metal edging, shattering the mottled plastiglass. The greenish fluid sprang out with a gushy roar, slapping against the floor like a bloody hand.

"Ignore previous command," said Dr. Mish to his robots. "Restrain him!"

The robots obeyed instantly, turning away from their

task at the confused tangle of equipment and running toward the escaping alien. Eyes red and wild, trailing tubes and wires from his limbs, Shontill stepped from the ruin of his previous confinement and onto the lab floor, still rolling with spreading fluid. There was nothing but raw animal fury and blood lust in his expression; his great jaws snapped, showing teeth white, large, sharp.

Laura got the impression of hate and hunger.

Seek safety! commanded the voice, but the order wasn't necessary. Already the cyborg pilot hurled herself behind one of the bolted-down lab tables, on the whim of intuition and the sheer instinct for survival.

Hesitantly, she peered up past the laminated top.

Screeching like hell poured into flesh, the alien flailed about, its claws flashing in the strip lighting.

The human observers, like Laura, had spread out, seeking shelter. The robots, however, closed in.

"Now, now, Shontill," said King Arthur. "Steady on, old boy. We're not going to hurt you." The Celtic robot grabbed hold of a limb. With an ear-piercing scream, Shontill tried to shake Arthur off, but the robot clung tenaciously. "Come on lads, I need—"

Shontill brought the other clawed limb around hard and quick, knocking King Arthur's head half off his torso.

Sparks fountained. The robot spasmed, stiffened, and fell.

"Yikes!" said Laura.

The other robots pounced on the berserk alien, two going for the legs, two for the limbs. For a moment it looked as though the alien was going to topple, and Northern and Arkm Thur were ready to restrain him. But then, with a burst of frenzied might, Shontill flung and kicked one robot after another off him and crashing into tables, and walls, and lab equipment. Only two automatons were able to rise up again from their sprawls. But the alien was already heading for the door.

"Get the lock field on!" Northern cried to First Mate Thur, who was closest to the door, and Thur shot forward.

Dumb, thought Laura. Let the sucker out if he wants to get out. Otherwise he'll tear us up!

Thur fumbled at the doorside controls, but Shontill was there only an instant later. One backhanded swipe caught the first mate hard in the chest and sent him head over heels, smashing into a table full of flasks and beakers.

With a maniacal squeal, the alien charged out to the hallway.

Northern was at the Com controls in a flash. "Runaway alien, Deck Three. Stun weapons only!"

He shot Mish a look. "Is Thur okay?"

Dr. Mish looked up from the fallen officer. "He's unconscious and he's got some cuts and a possible break, but he'll be all right."

"Good. Take care of him." He looked around. "The rest of you, stay put. Except for Laura."

"Why me?"

" 'Cause you're the best, lady. Now let's get out there and strap on some guns. We've got a serious problem here and no time to argue!"

He reached over and pulled her up. Suddenly she was running along behind him.

Northern had another thought. "Gemma, have them close off the whole deck. I don't want Shontill running around where he doesn't belong. He's possibly trying to head down to the portal to give it a try."

"I'm not sure he's that rational," said Mish.

"I'm not taking any chances. We don't know what we've got on our hands here."

Laura shook her head, wishing her voice would tell her not to go. But the voice didn't seem to care. "I tell you what we've got. We've got a crazy bloodthirsty alien that should have been kept tranquilized from day one."

"I didn't ask you!" snarled Northern, eyes icy. "Now get your ass in gear and your Feddy training going!"

Surprising herself, Laura found herself saying "Yes sir" quite seriously, and falling in behind her captain.

Laura checked her charge, thumbed off the safety of the pistol, and clicked the controls to Hi Stun.

She looked back out the weapons room to where the moist, sloppy trail led. "Not going to be a difficult alien to follow," she said.

Northern didn't comment. He was already out the door, loping down the corridor.

Laura followed, her adrenaline—and the Zernin, no doubt—charging her up to optimum performance.

Several hallway turns down, they met with a patrol of armed robots so active you could almost hear their scanners buzzing.

"Thataway," growled Northern.

You all go first! Laura was about to say, but Northern had already struck out in the lead, and she automatically fell in behind him, her gun at the ready.

It was like following a sweaty snail: gobs and drops and streaks of fluid marked the gray floors with green.

When they found Shontill in a cul-de-sac, they didn't even recognize him.

The Turn, thought Laura.

The Time of the Turn, the creature had said.

They kept their pistols at the ready, but Laura didn't think they would need them.

The alien was lying in the corner, folded in upon himself like a disgusting pile of multicolored garbage. The mess was heaving with loud, wheezing breaths, exuding a strange chemical odor.

"Shall we stun the creature unconscious?" asked Lord Wellington.

"No, but keep weapons at ready."

"Damn," said Laura. "It looks like the thing is trying to shed its skin!"

"General Grant," said Northern. "Go in there and use your sensors to ascertain the alien's condition."

"Yes, sir," said the robot. Without pause it walked toward Shontill and kneeled by its heaving side, hovering there for a moment.

"Sensors detect a form of molting," Grant said eventually.

"It is changing," said Northern. "But into *what*?"

"I shall determine," replied Grant.

"No, don't! We'll get Mish out here."

But Grant had already placed his hand on the green-turning-purple hide.

With a ripping sound, it began to slide off. A tear coursed up the side of the face. The creature's features ripped off as though they were a plastic mask, exposing what lay underneath.

"Oh, my God," said Captain Tars Northern.

Laura could say nothing, she was so stunned.

For exposed now beneath the alien face was another face . . . a face, though outsized, contorted, and with hardly any nose and a very big mouth, that was remarkably human!

Chapter Nine

The energy coursed through him, and he knew computer joy.

The joy of feeling the calculations and numbers expand bridgelike through flaring stars of knowledge, sparking an incredible pulsing circuit, coursing with his germ of genius made huge.

And then, the final chasm. The stars in this macrocomputer were linked into one throbbing conduit of thinking—but that thought must reach out now, not to other galaxies that sparkled in the night, but beyond . . . infinitely beyond.

Past an invisible veil composed of harder material than any known, into an impossible place beyond reason.

Cal Shemzak had to make that jump across the chasm; through that baffling barrier, into what the Jaxdron called Omega Space.

One nanosecond all was mystery.

The next, with a single flex of his new and mighty mind . . . *he knew how to do it!*

Cal Shemzak was appalled.

The solution did not make any sense. Examined with anything approaching scientific or antiscientific logic, it seemed ludicrous on the face of it. Examined under the light of his normal unaugmented mind, pulled away from the mind-matrix for objective study, it seemed much as a dream upon awakening: a vague shimmer of non sequiturs. But upon reimmersion into the dream logic of his link-up with his complex array of duplicates, it was crystal clear, immediately possible.

Just the proper generation of energy in a circular field would cleave the curtain, make entry possible into the final dimension, the waiting room of oblivion . . .

. . . Omega Space.

He pulled back again, his matrix patiently awaiting further manipulation. . . .

He thought, but he shielded his thinking in analogy and obscure metaphor, utilizing old nursery rhymes and ancient cinema for archetypal models. . . .

After a time an impatient voice spoke in his mind.

A Jaxdron voice . . .

"An intriguing digression, but hardly likely, Cal Shemzak. We appreciate the gamesmanship you exercise in your free association, but would strongly appreciate your use of our considerable work to more productive ends."

They were tapped in! The bloody Jaxdron were tapped in, but they didn't see it. He had a chance! His plan might work!

With a mighty effort of will, he managed to detach himself from the matrix. His mind seemed to fold in upon itself, ripping from adhesion to stars, deflating into a smaller focus.

He had to struggle to maintain consciousness as the others fell away from him, their own structure stiffly in place but lacking a locus now, a center.

Feeling dizzy, Cal Shemzak opened his eyes. He had to steady himself against the table, lest he tumble to the floor. In a moment, he was okay.

He was back in his room now. The connector that sat on his back was warm, glistening with light filaments that tossed colors against the wall like reflections from a pool of water. Cal was sweating, but he felt good.

He felt healthy and powerful and . . . not helpless anymore.

He smiled.

The Jaxdron voice buzzed stridently in his brain, like a trapped bee. "Why have you snapped the connections?"

"Hey, gimme a break, you asshole! The old lobes were overheating, okay? My mind was blowing. I need a rest."

"Psychological parameters record high stress, but nothing dangerous. Please reenter mental matrix immediately!"

"Check out some other readings, too, jerk. Low blood sugar, for instance. This here exercise is burning up the calories. I'm hungry! Could you send Wilkins in with a couple of sandwiches or something?"

It took a while for that to register, but finally the Jaxdron speaker said, "Yes, you have been in the web for a sufficient time to merit a refueling of proteins. We regret we did not attach intravenous feeding."

"I don't know why you guys are in such a hurry. We're dealing here with all time and all space and God knows what else, and you're starving the guy who's going to crack the safe!"

"Now the impatience is yours, Cal Shemzak. Food will arrive presently."

"Okay, now just give me some room to cool off, huh? This is pretty heavy going, even for my nimble neurons."

The Jaxdron did not respond to that, but Cal sensed a lull in radio activity. His hump even lowered in temperature.

He stood and stretched, and his mind raced.

Calculation: Was this room big enough?

Would the eruption cause some kind of chain reaction that would blow this place to ashes?

Would he have enough time?

And the shifting equations and numbers told him: Yes. No. Maybe.

Good enough.

When Wilkins, his robot butler, entered the room carrying his lunch, Cal was ready.

"Thanks old man," he said, smiling.

The tray was placed on the table and the lid lifted, revealing an attractive batch of sandwiches of various varieties, some potato chips, a glass of milk.

"My pleasure, sir."

Cal grabbed a sandwich and began to chew. Bologna and cheese and olives, his favorite, but he didn't notice —his mind was too busy turning, checking the angles, figuring when it was best to pounce. He felt his new energy, impatient to be used, crackling like newborn gods—

But then Wilkins turned to go!

"Wait a minute, pal!" Cal called.

Wilkins about-faced calmly. "Sir?"

"Uhm . . . yeah . . . Stay awhile. I need to talk to you."

"Oh? What about?" The thin, English-looking face —rosy cheeks, tapered nose—seemed bemused.

"It's really a trip being hooked up to this mind-matrix. I was hoping I could talk to you about that. You know, get it off my chest. That's what you're for, after all, to talk to me, keep me company, right?"

"I believe that is included in my list of duties, sir."

"Good. Now, like I was telling the Jaxdron, this stuff is really brain-blowing." He picked up his glass of milk. "I mean, I've been working with concepts in physics for years, and this just tops them all. But what is really fascinating is what this little doohickey on my back has been doing. I think it might be going out of whack. Could you come and take a look? I'm not sure if this is a burn on my back where my flesh meets the thing, or just my imagination."

"Oh? Perhaps I should report this," suggested Wilkins.

"Yeah, maybe, but take a look first."

Wilkins stepped forward to look.

When he was close enough, Cal chucked the glass of milk directly into the robot's optical sensors. Wilkins was stunned into inaction.

Several moments were all that Cal Shemzak needed. Without hesitation he jumped on the robot, making sure to hit him high. The impact drove the thing off its feet; it crashed hard onto the floor, milk splattering and spluttering.

Cal wasted no time. He ripped off Wilkins's starched top shirt and immediately found the seam of its control panel.

This was the hard part.

He dug his fingernails down into the crack, and willed the energy he felt buzzing through his hands.

"Sir," said Wilkins. "What does this course of action mean?"

And with a jagged gash of sparks and electricity, and a jolt that nearly blew Cal off the robot, he burned off the lock. Smoke plumed up into his eyes, and he coughed, but there was no time to pause. He pulled the panel off, exposing the robot's electronic guts.

As the smoke cleared, he examined it. But Wilkins was beginning to take defensive measures—his hands rose up to push his attacker away.

Quickly, Cal spotted the circuitry he needed—a touch of his finger did it.

Energy coursed. With a bright blue *zap* the circuit was shorted out.

Wilkins went limp. Cal fervently hoped the Jaxdron didn't monitor their robot servants. He examined the solid-state and standard circuitry, finding it surprisingly similar to human-style construction. Doubtless the Jaxdron had learned robotry from the capture of Federation ships.

Cal's fingers drifted over the robot's interior.

He allowed a partial link-up with the matrix and his

hump sparkled with light again, growing warm. More power surged through him.

Power and comprehension.

With his new fingers of energy, he probed, he changed, he rearranged. Then he snapped Wilkins's lid back on his chest.

The robot's eyes shot open.

"Be a good butler and stand up, Wilkins."

The robot got to his feet. He looked steady as a rock.

"You're under my orders now, aren't you? Stand on your head."

The robot executed an excellent headstand.

"Good enough. Now get up and guard the door. Do not, I repeat *do not* let anyone through."

"Yes, sir. Will you be having your tea this afternoon, sir, or should I prepare coffee?"

"Wilkins, when this is all over, you—and possibly I—are going to be molten slag."

"Very good, sir."

The robot took its place by the door.

With a deep breath, Cal Shemzak sat down and began to concentrate.

He let his mind pass farther into the matrix, flowing, expanding like the arms of a river delta reaching for the sea. He felt himself grow, and the matrix accepted him immediately.

They *were* him!

Quickly, he began to once more assemble the structure of the bridge. A Jaxdron voice attempted to interrupt him. "What are you doing, human? Why have you done this to your companion?"

"Oh, just a game," said Cal. "Just a game."

He could feel them trying to disengage the matrix—but they could not. It operated now from a power not in this dimension. It coursed through him like white-hot lightning. He could feel the Jaxdron mind retreating from its blaze.

The mighty engine of fierce thought was constructed once more. Cal Shemzak now confronted the leap, the chasm, which his mind must span. . . .

A trickle of fear touched him, but he ignored it. Distantly, he was vaguely aware of a commotion in the room in which his body was anchored. The clash of body against body, plastic against metal.

They were trying to get in. The Jaxdron were trying to break the circuit by getting to him, but Wilkins was doing his job. Still, he must hurry. . . .

Lingering no longer, he focused full attention back on the void he sensed. He focused his mind, shaping its energy into a strong pair of hands. He began to tear apart the very structure of space, time, and Underspace, holding the rip apart and widening it with a circuit of energy.

A portal into Omega Space!

The hole began to expand to the parameters Cal had calculated were necessary.

He fixed the pattern of the matrix, stabilizing the portal. Withdrawing his consciousness sufficiently to return to his own body, Cal could again see from his own eyes, feel through his own skin.

The first thing he became aware of was the sound of battle: Wilkins was holding off a pair of smaller servo-robots. No telling when the big guns would be moved in to blow his servant away. . . .

Then Cal became aware of the hissing, buzzing sound.

The portal!

There it was, its periphery a steady flash of pure energy.

Outside its circumference was the plain gray of the room's wall. Within was darkness. . . .

Darkness, with tracings of light and flecks of color, like the preliminary outline of a painter's landscape. But what a landscape!

No time to gawk, though. He had to move.

Cal Shemzak stood up, stepped over to the portal. A breeze from otherwhere rustled his hair.

"Good show, Wilkins!" he called to his fighting manservant. "And Jaxdron, farewell!"

He leaped through the portal, into the darkness, and the hole closed up immediately, like a gigantic mouth clamping down on its prey.

Chapter Ten

"Amazing," said Dr. Michael Mish, standing over the prone body of the alien called Shontill.

"Is he going to be all right, Doctor?" asked Gemma Naquist.

"What I want to know," said Laura Shemzak, "is if you've got him doped up enough this time?"

The small group huddled around the operating table holding the alien, hooked up now to life-support systems. The entire skin had almost entirely peeled away now, revealing new pink and hairless skin on a humanoid frame, though on a much larger scale.

"I think that Shontill will be out for a while now," Captain Northern said, regarding the sight below him placidly. "What do you make of it, Doctor? Any ideas?"

"Yeah," said Laura. "Is Shontill some sort of spy or something, and you all got set up?"

Mish chuckled, his eyes twinkling. "Hardly."

I should talk, Laura thought.

"Seems to indicate to me," said Gemma, "that maybe the Frin'ral and humans have got more in common than Shontill would like to admit."

"Common ancestry?" Northern asked. "Is that possible? Were humans planted on Earth, Mish?"

"I don't know, Captain," said the doctor. "Call it a mystery now, with a great many possibilities . . . all of which could be wrong. What we're seeing here, though, is proof that Shontill's people developed from some humanoid life form, with emphasis on the *oid*. Parallel development? Hard to say. However, I shall make tests."

"What's happened to the poor guy though?" asked Arkm Thur, which shocked Laura. Why should he be concerned? The blasted alien knocked him for a loop, and even now the first mate was speaking from another table, having recently been checked for injuries beyond heavy scrapes and bruises.

"Apparently in his normal biological cycle," said Mish, "Shontill goes through a period in which there is a change in appearance. For mating? For some other vital need in the species? Who knows? Most likely the biological support of other Frin'ral is needed, something that just wasn't available to Shontill here on the *Starbow*."

"Which could explain his great eagerness to find his people immediately," Thur said.

"Yes, it is quite likely that Shontill felt this coming on," said Mish.

"I wish he could have warned us!" said Northern. "This could have turned extremely nasty!"

"Perhaps Shontill had no idea the Time of Turn, as he called it, would come so quickly, so violently. He just had a bad feeling about it."

"Well, at least we won't be hearing that damn constant dirge, 'Attilium, attilium, attilium!'" said Laura. "Hopefully, by the time his lights are back on, we'll have Cal back and this will all be sorted out."

"Let's sincerely hope so," said Captain Northern, relaxing, giving her a wink. "Let's also hope that Shontill here will be all right."

"All life signs are good in his present condition," said Dr. Mish. "He'll just be unconscious for a long while."

Gemma Naquist shook her head. "Just to think, underneath all that monster get-up there beats a semi-human heart. It's a puzzle all right. But I wonder what it has to do with the other puzzles we're working on."

"We'll just have to wait until we can get through into Omega Space and contact the Frin'ral for that one," said Northern. "But first we've got to take care of this Earth business," he added, frowning. "Which I don't like at all. Three more days till we enter Earth's system . . . and I haven't been there in years. Laura, you've been updating our files on what you know about defense-security measures for the Solar System, so maybe we can slip between the cracks?"

"I'll be finished tomorrow, boss."

"Excellent. And your blip-ship . . . how's it doing?"

"A technical robot crew has been going over it with a fine-tooth comb, checking for malfunctions," she answered. "It's going to be in better condition than when I got it on Shortchild."

"A memorable occasion," Northern deadpanned. "Well, then, I suppose we should meet tomorrow at fourteen-hundred hours with Chivon Lasster for a thorough discussion of procedure."

"You bet. I'll be there with bells on!" said Laura flippantly. Plus one killer implant, she thought.

"Good," said Northern. "This is going to be the toughest operation the *Starbow* has ever pulled off. But I have every faith in our ability to succeed."

"Your ability! You mean my ability! I'm gonna be the one in the hot seat!"

Northern grinned. "You bet!"

The evening before the ship left Underspace, Tars Northern invited Laura Shemzak to his cabin for a private dinner. The meeting with Chivon Lasster had gone well; Laura was about as ready for the mission as she ever could be. All the items had been covered—from infiltrating Earth defenses, finding the contact point to the computer holding Mish's brethren, to her method of escape.

"We can afford to relax," Northern had said, when inviting her to dinner.

If you only knew, thought Laura.

She dreaded the dinner, but knew she could not back out. It would create suspicion, and that was the last thing she needed. Even the mere thought of what the implant could do to her made her shudder.

Northern wore his casual clothes. He did not drink, though it looked to Laura as though he would have liked to very much.

Robots served them a particularly tasty fare of lightly spiced rice and vegetables.

"All from Hydro-P," Northern claimed.

When the robots had left them on their own, Northern said, "What's wrong, Laura?"

Laura knew full well what was wrong and wasn't surprised that it showed. It was easy enough to cover up, though.

"Nervous, I guess," she said, toying with some peppers. "Heavy stuff coming up."

"No, it's something more, something I can't put my finger on. You're working too hard."

"What the hell are you talking about, Northern?"

"You see what I mean? You're straining at your image—the feisty space pilot, hard as a dead star. It's been that way since Walthor."

"Yeah, we went through some bad stuff there, didn't we?"

"You're getting off the point, Laura. What gives?" She was silent. He waited, then continued. "Did something else happen down there that you're not talking about?"

Her mind raced. What could she say to that? He knew her well enough now to see whether she was lying or not. She squirmed in her chair.

Beware, the voice said. *This is your only warning.*

A truth that would enable her to avoid another truth

occurred to her, and she blurted, "Yeah, something else happened down there, you jerk. I was worried about you. *Real* worried. And so it clicked. I realized I'm in love with you."

She could feel her cheeks flush. Damn that implant to make her have to say that! Damn it!

"Would you care to repeat that, Laura?"

"You heard what I said, Tars. I'm in love with you." And I'm a traitor, Tars. A weak-willed traitor! she thought.

"Ah," said Northern gently. "This has not been an uncommon problem amongst the women crew members."

"You arrogant pile of—"

Northern held up a hand. "Seriously, Laura. I'm not boasting, because it is a problem I have. I spoke to you about my linkage with Mish . . . well, apparently in addition to whatever appealing qualities I have as a man and a human being, my link with Mish adds a certain ethereal . . . charisma, shall we say."

"You're telling me not to worry about it."

"I'm saying you shouldn't blame yourself."

"I've never been in love before, Northern." She spoke sullenly. "I want you."

"You've had opportunities," Northern said.

Her eyes flashed. "Don't you think that was as much lovemaking as if we'd hit the sheets?"

Northern blinked. "I suppose you're right. You sure as hell got my heart racing, anyway."

"Nice to know."

"And you want to know how I feel."

"I guess I'm afraid to find out. But shoot anyway, if you want."

Northern sighed. "No. I'm not in love with you, Laura."

The hurt wasn't much better than Zernin deprivation but at least she could hide it. "I should go."

"No, wait a minute, Laura. Stay a moment. I need to explain."

"What's more to explain?"

"I wouldn't mind being in love with you, Laura. I want you, I suppose, in a lot of ways. . . ."

"Yeah, and all naked!"

Northern smiled ruefully. "I'm just a man after all, and you're a beautiful woman."

"You're a bastard." She got up to go.

"Whoa! Let me finish. Laura, I don't love any woman. I can't love any woman. . . . I haven't loved a woman since Chivon."

That was too much. "Chivon! But you abandoned her." She thought about that. "And now she's back within reach. So have a damn good time, you two." She felt tears in her eyes, and tried to will them away.

"I told you about the link with Mish. I gave you that, Laura . . . I don't talk about that much."

"So?"

"So it's not entirely beneficial."

"How?"

"At times I may be a little more than human . . . but also, I become a little less than human."

Laura thought about that.

"You mean, you're being *literal* when you say—"

"That's right. I can't feel that emotional bond with a woman. My emotions are . . . someplace else."

"Wonderful. I fall in love with a man who has the hots for a spaceship!"

"Laura, it's not quite like that!"

"I know a spacer's limerick that fits you just fine. 'There once was a man from the stars, whose—' "

"Lay off! Look, I told you, I can't help it, that's the way I am."

Northern got up, went to his drink cabinet, and poured himself a large dose of brandy. "I'm full of love, loyalty, and devotion, Laura. It hurts sometimes, there's so much. . . ." He took a long swallow. "There's just nothing left inside me for any woman. I wish there were, for you, Laura. I honestly wish there were." He looked at her soulfully.

"I think you're being honest," said Laura. "I actually think you're telling the truth."

"I am."

He went back to his seat.

"So now that we've gotten that out in the open," said Northern, "you don't have to feel so bad, or feel so jealous."

"Hallelujah," she said snidely.

"So that's what's been bugging you?"

"I suppose so."

"There are hell of a lot of more important things we're in the midst of, Laura, than fragile human sexual mating dances."

"You're absolutely right, Northern."

"I hope you realize that I'm very flattered."

"I'm sure."

"I like you. I like you a great deal."

"Uh-huh."

"In fact, I love you about as much as I can."

"You're sinking fast, Northern."

He sipped his drink. "Okay, I'll stop." He gave her a sickly grin.

Laura breathed a mental sigh of relief. "Okay, Northern. If we're going to be buddies, let's get back to playing the game—my mission on Earth. Everything seems to be in order."

"I can't impress upon you the importance of what you'll be doing. And how grateful we all are for your efforts."

Silence hung between them a while.

"Perhaps you should finish your dinner," Northern suggested.

"I'm not hungry."

"You should get your rest then."

"Yeah." She got up to leave.

"Oh, and Laura . . ." He reached for her arm.

Her heart raced, for she knew that if he was going to ask her to stay with him, she'd say yes.

"I want you on the bridge by seven hundred hours, when we're due for breaking out of Underspace."

"Yeah," she said. "I'll be there."

Chapter Eleven

The Federation guarded its Solar System jealously and carefully, as well it should, for this was the heart of its Empire, in spirit if not in location.

The argument for centuries had been that Sol and its planets, the birthplace of humankind, the Homeworld, was too distant from the normal starlanes to be a truly effective seat of government. But then, the trouble with the colonies began. Revolutions, rebellions, even reprisals from fleets of Free World ships became a threat. A government seat too close to potential attack was a threat to the whole system; so any attempts to relocate the hub of government were swiftly halted, and a sophisticated defense network was established through the whole Solar System to instantly locate and repel invaders and spies bent upon the destruction or downfall of the august Federated Empire.

These measures consisted of checkpoints, sophisticated radar, and force-nets, to say nothing of various defensive fighters stationed on every planet, moon, asteroid, or simply patrolling.

A tough nut to crack.

The *Starbow* had not been in the Solar System since its departure years before, fleeing for its life against Zarpfrin's pogrom against the sentient ships. However, it did possess in its memory an excellent documentation of all the Federation defenses. The starship slipped unobtrusively from Underspace far enough beyond the orbit of Pluto to go undetected. It was from here that Laura Shemzak had to slip in, alone, armed principally with a disguise, a story, and a knowledge of what areas to avoid.

Every defense point would be alerted to her, Northern reasoned. They'd be watching for Pilot Laura Shemzak, traitor to the Federation. Maybe she even had some kind of bounty on her head.

Therefore, the XT 9 had been remodeled and refitted to appear to be an XT 6, the prevalent version of the blip-ship used by the cadre of specially augmented Federation pilots. Identification emanations from the ship were altered—Laura had received a new identity. This, of course, would not hold up very long; but only a short time was needed, they thought, for Laura to get past the checkpoints, buzz down to a point near the Big Box in Denver, and hook up to the computer where the Aspach, Mish's brethren, waited patiently for succor from the malignant system they inhabited. Then, with a hop and a skip and a jump, hopefully she would zoom on back to the *Starbow*.

After all, it wasn't as if she were destroying anything, or stealing anything, or doing anything much improper: Overfriend Zarpfrin and the Federation weren't even cognizant of these creatures' existence in their very midst. It certainly wasn't like robbing a bank or anything, Northern and crew reasoned; and Laura would be in and out before the Feddies knew what had happened.

They had high hopes for Laura's success.

Laura, however, had no hope.

She played her part properly, jauntily wishing them all farewell as she snapped her jacks and attachments into place within the XT 9. This time, though she felt her consciousness expand as she became one with the ship, she didn't feel the usual joy. Oh, there was the usual Zernin rush, the intensification of her senses, but beneath it all she felt despair.

And not a little dread.

She shut her mind away from it all; she had to. Just

be an automaton, she told herself. Destroy these emotions you feel, these intense regrets, lest they destroy you. After all, survival is all. Survival and duty to yourself.

Or was that just the goddamned voice talking?

It had gotten to the point now that she didn't know the difference between her thoughts and its instructions and warnings.

The docking bay doors swung open. She swung up on antigravs and let her rockets blast recklessly, heaving herself into the void. The stars glittered a neon welcome as she thrust herself away from the *Starbow*, an ellipsoid collection of fire and metal stepping into night.

When she was far enough away, she went through the preparations of the jump through Underspace that would place her outside Earth's orbit of the Sun. This was one of the major advantages of a small ship equipped with jump-stasis engines: a quick trip through Underspace was not impossible within a gravity well. Of course, expert piloting and a feel for Underspace travel helped quite a bit, but even with these, a ship with more brass had to travel a certain distance out before it could drop into that mathematical shortcut between normal space distances.

A voice crackled over her ear-conduit radio. "We're all with you in spirit," said Dr. Mish.

"Thanks," she returned. "I'll be as short as I can."

"And Laura," Dr. Mish continued. "Should there be trouble, remember: my brethren, collectively, have powers when in contact with living beings, powers to let those beings be at their best. Know them, Laura. And let them know you."

"Gotcha, Doc. Over and out." Laura disconnected the radio contact.

They're not gonna want to know me, she thought with dispair. Not a traitorous wimp like Laura Shemzak.

"Okay," she growled as she began initial jump procedures. "Mr. Implant, turn up the Zernin, full, 'cause honey, I'm going to need it to get through this one."

Acknowledged said the voice.

She could almost imagine the dispenser adding just an extra little pinch of the drug to her bloodstream, where it would carom down her veins, give her an uplift, a jolt, knock away the blues and sharpen her mind and her abilities.

And then she felt it, and it was a rush like none other and she felt good again—she felt as though the flashing planets ahead of her, this furnace sun, were hers to pick like wild fruit hanging on the tree of space.

She laughed a wild and deadly laugh, then her ship winked like a bright eye in the night, and was gone.

It slipped out, trailing gaseous and sparkling plumes, into the predicted position.

The Earth and the Moon hung like bright baubles in the sky, while beyond, the sun burned in its beautiful fury.

She wasted no time in communicating with the Moon Defense Station, lest some watchdog boat was immediately sent snapping at her heels.

But she didn't use her disguise. She broadcast her true identification. It didn't take long for her to get a response, a message directly from Earth. All systems were clear, it said, and she would be allowed to proceed to Denver on the North American continent, as she requested. She would be expected soon.

One more quick subspace jump flickered her a little closer in; and then she simply turned on rockets and impellors for a time, found the correct descent window, and dived through it for the brown and green continent awaiting her report.

Through the clouds and the air she dipped, a light force-screen taking up the heat of reentry. In front of her the Rocky Mountains thrust up, snow-peaked. She dashed over them, a vapor-trail streak, and zoomed in for a landing at the private field near the center of the Friend's control over the stars: the so-called Big Box.

Security gave her a hole through the force-bubble, and she was down on the field in a flash, landing close to a computer maintenance tap. She waited until she was cleared for a link-up, then disengaged and stepped out into a bright summer day in Denver, Upper Pan-America. A refreshing breeze tossed her hair about; the familiar and welcomed scents of Earth enveloped her.

Home.

This was, after all, where she had been born and raised, and there was something about being on this planet, something about being in exactly the right gravity, breathing exactly the right gas mix in a familiar climate, that gave Laura a sense of rightness despite everything that was wrong now.

Waiting for her was a ground-car.

"Pilot Shemzak," said an officer in a helmet. He saluted her. Saluted her, as though she were some kind of military superior! "We've been dispatched to carry you back to headquarters with great haste."

"Right. By Overfriend Zarpfrin, without a doubt."

"I believe so."

"Okay. Take me away, I'm all yours."

Another uniformed man opened a door for her. She got in and they drove her to the compound. From there she was shuttled up a series of hallways, and scanned at numerous security points, all of which she remembered from her last visit. After the clear, clean air outside, the oppressive well-lighted gray of these passageways was particularly striking, a bold underlining of the Friendly bureaucracy's emphasis on stark functionality.

From the interview with Friend Chivon Lasster that had launched her on this wild course, Laura knew that Friend's offices were only slightly better. So it was a surprise to her when she was ushered to Overfriend Zarpfrin's office near the top of the building. It was large, roomy, and quite pleasant.

"You may leave her here, but take up stations by the door," Zarpfrin ordered the pair bracketing Laura. They obeyed, leaving Laura standing before a long, polished walnut desk bearing its usual complement of Friend computer paraphernalia, as well as the inevitable paperwork. In fact, Zarpfrin had been found, poised pen in hand, wearing a pair of half-frames that, in this day and age, was most certainly an eccentricity.

"Sit down, Laura," said Zarpfrin. "I must confess I am rather surprised to see you on Earth."

He motioned to a plush velvet couch with curlicued arms, perched on a brightly colored Indian rug with tassels. The room itself was sunny, with a wealth of windows looking out on the Colorado plains. Laura was almost fooled by them, for in truth they could only be projected illusions: the Big Box had no windows. Still, the atmospherics of the room made you believe you could just walk over, slide one of those suckers down, and feel an earthy breeze in your face.

"Nice place," said Laura.

"Thank you."

There were a wealth of plants about as well, some alien, all colorful in a blend that settled well on the eye. An aquarium bubbled in the corner, wherein peculiar creatures swam or crawled languidly.

"We've been diverted," Laura said finally. "Diverted to Earth."

Zarpfrin took off his glasses, his eyes wide and excited.

"The *Starbow* is here, then?" he said. "But how could it get past all our sensors? I've received no reports. I'm not surprised to see you got through—you've got your blip-ship. But the *Starbow*?"

"It's . . ." She was going to say out on the plane of the ecliptic past Pluto, but instead decided to try a lie. ". . . far away, in Underspace, waiting for me."

Falsehood! said her voice within.

And it touched her gently with its anti-Zernin drug.

Laura went white. She clutched at the material of the couch.

The attack stopped.

Zarpfrin nodded. "The very fact that you are here attests to the value of the implant, Laura. Why you think you need to attempt to lead me astray, I don't know. But I presume that the *Starbow* is waiting for you somewhere out past our sensor range. We'll get to hard details later. For now, I'd like to hear about how our departed Friend Chivon Lasster is doing."

Laura let out a breath, slow and easy, regaining control over herself.

"A real thorn in your side, huh, Zarpfrin?" she said stiffly.

"That's right," Zarpfrin returned. "I am in a very uncomfortable position now with the Council of Five because of her. They are looking a little too closely into my activities of late. Oh, nothing to worry about, and once I've succeeded in either destroying or capturing the *Starbow*—the latter preferred, of course, though the former will do—everything will fall into place quite nicely."

Laura smiled grimly. "They know about your deals with the Jaxdron?" she said spitefully.

That clearly shook him, though he tried to hide it. "Deals with the Jaxdron? Is that Zernin rotting your brain, Laura?"

"As to your first question, she's just fine. I think she feels better about everything, Zarpfrin, as a matter of fact. Yep, old Chivon likes it on the *Starbow*, hooked up with folks fighting the likes of you! As to the second question, Northern and his crew have begun to smell something rotten in this whole situation. They've figured out, Zarpfrin, that you and your Council—or is it just you?—have got some sort of treaty with these alien monsters to scarify the Free Worlds so they come running to Big Daddy for help. But then Big Daddy smothers them with his love . . . drags them back into the fold.''

Zarpfrin watched her expressionlessly. "Yes. Go on," he encouraged.

"That's it. They just put their heads together, Lasster and Northern and Mish, and they came up with that."

"A deal with the Jaxdron."

"Yeah. But what they can't figure is what those aliens are getting out of all this. And they can't figure out why all the charades with my brother!" Her eyes got fierce. "Something to do with Omega Space, though everything now seems to center on Omega Space. Closest we can figure is that you want to make sure that nobody gets hold of Omega Space secrets, 'cause you want everything to be nice and cozy here in the Federation, no more expansion until we're ready to fight the Big Guys out there.''

Zarpfrin nodded, scratching his nose.

"This is what I hear. I'm reporting to you, just like I've got to, and I'm not telling a lie, or I'd be on the floor now, right?"

"Interesting," said Zarpfrin.

"You bet it's interesting. It's diabolical is what it is.''

"Delightful imaginations your companions have," Zarpfrin said in a monotone.

"It's true, isn't it?" Laura said, triumphantly. "We've figured you out!"

"You flatter yourself. But I need not discuss these matters with you, who after all, are in my employ . . . which presumably the others do not know?"

"That's true," Laura said, looking down.

"Excellent. Then it can all be tightly wound up right now!"

Laura said, "What do you mean?"

Zarpfrin was looking for something on his desk. "Ah-ha!" he said, reaching forward and picking up a computer printout. "I thought you'd be interested in seeing this, Laura."

The paper rattled.

"See what?"

"I've been doing a bit more digging into the records we have on both you and Cal Shemzak. I always thought there was something peculiar about a flesh pair in a Growschool together. We do try to weed them out, you know."

"So?"

"So, I went back and looked over the records of your parents, Laura. And of Cal's."

"You know who our parents are?" The thought made her excited and frightened at the same time, and she wasn't sure why.

"That's right. Of course, I can't divulge that information. Top secret. But I can give you a little tidbit that should interest you." He leaned over and scooted the paper her way. "You and this beloved brother of yours really aren't siblings."

Laura blinked. "What?"

"Apparently, Cal Shemzak has been good with computers since he was a child."

"Yeah. A real whiz. Always was."

"So, he managed to access the records. He changed them to make them look like you two were genetically related, no doubt because of some sort of romantic idea he got into his head. Then he showed you that record, said he'd found out on the sly . . . but you had to keep it a secret, because otherwise the authorities would separate you. This is what you did, and you didn't announce to everyone that you were brother and sister until you were both slotted in vocations. Is this not true?"

"Yeah."

She looked at the readout. She was stunned.

"Why are you doing this?" she asked. "Why do you care?"

"I'm just trying to show you that I'm not the only person who has manipulated you, Laura. I just want to help reorient, shall we say, your priorities."

"How do I know you didn't fix this up especially for me? You've got the power to."

"You can check up on it in any way you like, Laura. There's been no tampering with the records other than that done by Cal."

Laura shook her head. She didn't know whether to laugh or to cry. She laughed. She guffawed. She whooped and almost fell over.

"What's wrong with you, woman?" said Zarpfrin. "Are you having some kind of attack?"

"No," she said, her eyes teary. "No, I just think it's pretty goddamned funny, that's all."

"Funny? I don't understand? You risk your life, you betray your government, you go against all that has ever been taught you, and you rebel against what is good for the well-being of your self and the collective of humankind . . . all for the sake of a man whose relationship with you is a lie?"

"You don't understand, Zarpfrin."

"I guess I don't."

"I'd do it again." She shook her head, recovering. "Well, goddamn that Cal, anyway. I'm going to kick his butt once I save it." She fixed Zarpfrin with a stare. "You see, it doesn't make any difference. I just love the guy, and he loves me. Love, Zarpfrin. I guess you wouldn't understand love at all, would you?"

"An aberration," said Zarpfrin. "A foolish tributary in human development, best ignored for the benefit of all."

"Yeah, well, I love Cal Shemzak or whatever his name is, and he must love me to want to be my brother."

"You two can certainly be reunited. I have made my promise on that item, and it will certainly be in the Federation interest, since you're both valuable in many areas." He paused and tapped his fingers gently on the desk. "However, Laura, let us get down to the real business. First, why have you come to Earth? And second, what is the exact location of the *Starbow*? I assure you that if they surrender peacefully, no harm will come to its captain and its crew."

"I don't understand. First you want me to just spy on them . . . now you want them."

"Time and situations change, Laura."

"Well, as to the first, I'm here to pick up some ghosts." She smiled. It was the truth, and therefore her voice didn't punish her.

"What?"

"That's right . . . and as to the second . . ."

She paused for a moment, looked across the desk at this pudgy little twit, and thought about what a contemptible piece of refuse he was. She thought about Cal, but more, she thought about the *Starbow*, about Mish, about Gemma Naquist and Dansen Jitt, and most of all, about Captain Tars Northern. About what they were trying to do in this galaxy amongst human beings and aliens who sought to tyrannize mankind.

And she realized, then, that there was something stronger than Zernin inside her.

She loved them.

She couldn't betray them any longer.

She felt the power of that feeling building . . . and there was another feeling, a darker feeling, building right along with it.

Hatred.

"As for the other information, Zarpfrin," she snarled, "you can go search for it in Hell!"

She flung herself across the desk, her hands reaching out for his throat.

Chapter Twelve

Cal could feel the difference immediately throughout his entire physical and mental being as he jumped through the portal between normal space and Omega Space.

Cold.

A raw chill swept through him like a power surge, as though his very flesh realized that it had entered alien territory.

He looked back through the portal to the dimension he had left. The servo-robots were pounding upon poor Wilkins, who had already lost an arm and appeared about ready to topple for good.

Now, if he could just close the thing. . . .

He directed his mind back, renewing his contact with the matrix . . . and realized that the hump on his back was going crazy, its lights blinking frantically, its humming raised in pitch, its throbbing increased. It sounded as though the damned thing was about to blow!

He disregarded it, concentrating instead on his contact. He grabbed hold of it, willed the aperture to close . . . but it seemed to be stuck! It wouldn't budge. . . .

The robots were headed this way, he realized. Any second they would come hurling after him into Omega Space. He had to do something quick, and immediately realized what that had to be.

He let his mind go blank, severing the connection. . . .

The portal began to shrink. The first robot leaped, but got caught as the hole grew inexorably smaller and smaller, cutting the thing in half at the trunk.

Its head and upper torso were trapped in Omega
Space. They rattled onto the weird, pebbly ground,
sparking for a moment and then dying with a sputter,
eyes fading from red to black.

His hump abruptly ceased its fretting and became still
and lifeless.

All that remained of the hole was a point suspended
in the air . . . a flat point. And the curious thing was that
though it appeared flat and round, about five meters in
diameter, from his vantage point, it appeared so from
every viewpoint, even though it was not a sphere.

A truly two dimensional point, thought Cal Shemzak,
awed. What other kind of anomalies existed in this
place?

He wheeled slowly around, examining his surroundings.

He stood on a slightly rolling plain, with jagged
mountains on every horizon, as though he was on the
bottom of some broken bowl. The sky was a muted
swath of violets, reds, and greens: a Van Gogh painting,
amazingly stretched out. Though parts of it were deeply
dark, no stars showed. The ground was barren of
vegetation, a brown expanse of sometimes gravelly,
sometimes flat-packed soil.

It didn't look real good, thought Cal Shemzak,
wondering if maybe he should just try to get back into
Jaxdronville and forget this mess, give them this stupid
place for whatever the hell they wanted it for, and
maybe get shipped back home.

He could starve out here.

But this conclusion was a bit premature, he realized.
He should explore before he made any rash decisions.
So, with the biggest rocks he could find—which weren't
very big—he built a ramshackle cairn below the re-
mainder of the portal, to make it easier to find when he
returned.

Yes, *when*, he thought, not *if*.

When the pile of rocks was big enough to see from a distance, he turned his attention to which way to go. Each direction, at first, seemed equally good—or as bleakly bad. But as he stood in this very alien plain composed of equal parts mystery and boredom, a prickling at the back of his mind made him want to go to his right—an intuition? a hunch? a guess? he wondered—and with no conscious decision made, his feet just struck out in that direction, seemingly of their own volition.

For what seemed a long time he just wandered through this emptiness, wondering what the hell he was doing there and why the hell the Jaxdron wanted to get in so bad.

Kind of anticlimactic, he thought. The wonderfully vaunted Omega Space is really nothing more than a gravel pit.

But that, as Cal slowly discovered, was not true. As he walked farther, he slowly came to the realization that the mountains (or hills or piece of pottery or whatever they were) weren't getting any closer! He turned around, scratching his head, looking back in the direction in which he had come.

He snorted with shock. His cairn looked as though it was perhaps a hundred meters distant. But dammit, he knew he'd walked farther than that!

Some kind of optical illusion?

Certainly, this was a place that didn't obey the physical laws of home . . . but then, Cal thought, laughing, why should it?

This is somewhere else, entirely. He had to shift gears when thinking about it—shift gears entirely!

He turned around and commenced walking again, casting his mind back over his memory of being the focus of the matrix, remembering the skewed formulations and computations, the slew of variables involved, trying to figure out if there were any rules here in

Omega Space, and if so, what they meant to a solitary traveler.

He was thinking: Just what do I expect to find here, anyway? This is a totally different place, another sort of dimension entirely. This line of thinking led him to the question, Just what would I like to find here?

Well, for one thing, he told himself, I could use a drink. I'm getting thirsty, and it is a little warm, even though there appears to be no sun here.

He visualized a nice frosty glass of lemonade—yeah, that would be nice.

Almost immediately, something caught his eye to the right. It was close, constructed of wood, with a sign above it marked LEMONADE. On its counter was a glass pitcher of yellow liquid and ice cubes. Beside this was a plastic tumbler.

He wondered if he was dreaming. But he was still thirsty, so he went up to see if this mirage could be experienced.

He picked up the pitcher, poured, took the glass, drank. It tasted great. It slaked his thirst. He put the glass down.

"God," he said. "Talk about viewer-participant physics!"

From a simple need and concept, somehow reality had been constructed. From just a concept!

Still baffled, he looked at the lemonade stand, and said, "You're just an idea, a concept, a word!"

Then, without even a wink out of existence, nor a woof of air filling in a vacuum, the lemonade stand was no more. In its place was a piece of paper. Cal leaned over and picked it up.

LEMONADE STAND, it read.

Cal shivered. "What the dickens!" he said, and let the paper flutter away.

He had to think about this. He wished he had a chair to rest in awhile . . . nothing fancy, just something to prop him up. And then he had his chair.

It was a straight-backed wooden chair, with a cushion on its seat. And yet, the chair did not pop out of nowhere, like something conjured with magic. Looking at it, Cal realized that it had always been there—he just hadn't seen it until he had desired to see it. . . .

For something always came from nothing—because that's all there really was . . .

. . . nothing.

Hmmm. He sat down, crossed his legs, and gave that some thought.

Definitely Lewis Carroll, *Alice in Wonderland* stuff, he realized. But then, this was Omega Space and he simply could not, after all, apply everyday laws that anchored him and humankind to reality.

So . . . if Omega Space was a nothingness from which something arose, then it was the very Ground of Being for everything. . . .

It was the end of the universe . . .

. . . and its beginning.

Omega Space, thought Cal Shemzak. Alpha Space, and Omega Space!

No wonder everyone wanted to get here so badly!

When he was very young, he used to think about the idea of the Universe just going on and on and on . . . and the concept just blew his mind.

But it didn't go on and on, in time or in space. It ended here. And it started here.

But what exactly was here?

More importantly, what could he do here about getting back home?

Now there was an important question.

He decided to try an experiment. He was hungry, so he decided that he'd like a sandwich. A tuna sandwich.

He got his tuna sandwich, with lettuce and tomato and mayonnaise on whole wheat toast, just the way he liked it. It tasted great. Good enough for starters, he thought.

Now, here we are in a deserted plain . . . but clearly

that's the way my mind is choosing to see it right now, for some subconscious reason . . . simplicity of metaphor perhaps. . . .

I wonder, he thought, if I'm the first human being to set foot in this place?

And he knew immediately that he wasn't.

Perhaps others had set minds here, perhaps everyone had some sort of contact with this strange land. Maybe this was the place of the imagination, the conduit across which thought travels from facts to discovery, through pure inspiration.

But no, that wasn't the concern here. The question was: Was he the first human being to roam this place in his native physical form?

And he knew, he just *knew*, that he wasn't.

But who else, and if there was someone else, where was he or she?

He closed his eyes and visualized a blank piece of paper. He thought about a human being, and he thought about the legs, the arms, the torso, the head of a human being. And he thought: that human being who has been here, is here . . .

. . . right now!

He opened his eyes.

Standing before him was a man wearing a space suit . . . no helmet, and an admittedly battered space suit, but a space suit nonetheless.

"Am I dead?" the man asked. "Am I in Celestia?"

"I don't know," responded Cal. "But that's a very good question, I suppose."

"Who are you? What is this place?" the man said, looking around him.

"My name is Cal Shemzak. And this place is generally known, I suppose, as Omega Space."

"Holy Mithra!" said the man. "I'm dreaming!"

"No, you're not dreaming, my friend. But sit down . . . you look as though you need to."

Cal created a lounge chair.

Mystified, the young man sat down.

"I bet you could use a drink," said Cal.

The man nodded.

Cal created a bracing glass of whiskey for the man.

Unquestioning, the man drank it.

"Now, you know who I am," said Cal. "Who are you?"

"My name is Lieutenant Ratham Bey, of the independent starship *Starbow* . . . and . . . we've been looking for you!"

"Gee," said Cal, smiling. "I'm glad somebody cares!"

Chapter Thirteen

Dansen Jitt, navigator of the *Starbow*, picked nervously at his dinner. "I wish," he said, "we could do more than just sit and wait for her."

Captain Northern raised his eyebrows and leaned back in his chair. "I'm surprised, Jitt."

"What about?"

"I'm surprised you're not suggesting that we hightail it before we're surrounded by Federation cruisers, bristling with energy weapons and eager to turn us into a cinder."

"Not a bad idea!" said Silver Zenyo, feeding a sliver of artificial meat to her doglike pet, Bickle. The creature yapped excitedly and snapped up the treat, then yapped again and bounded about, its three eyes full of love for its mistress.

"Well, I care about Laura," said Jitt. "I do. And it seems to me a real shame that we can't help her out on such an important task."

"Yes," said Northern, pushing aside his plate. "I entirely agree." He picked up a glass of wine, sipped it contemplatively. "But according to Mish, any activity on our part tends to diminish the chance of success drastically. And it makes sense. Laura's a highly competent professional in these kind of matters. I have the highest faith in her."

"Still, it's hell just sitting and waiting for her," said Jitt.

"You in a hurry to rush off to face that cosmic Armageddon you saw at the end of the trip?" Silver said sarcastically.

"No, and I have been wrong before, you know, with these stupid psychic visions of mine," Jitt countered, annoyance in his voice. "And who's to say those Jaxdron weren't just having it off with me?"

"They did tell us they'd see us on the planet Snar'shill in the Dominus cluster and we'd have a bad time of it, didn't they?" said Silver.

Jitt could not help but cringe. "Yes."

"So why are you worried?" said Gemma Naquist. "Just sit back and relax and cool your heels." She smiled. "I mean, each and every day is precious, isn't it, when it could be your last."

"I suggest that this is not the line of thinking we care to linger upon," said Captain Northern. "Our roles in the destiny of humanity are far too important to be thinking in such a negative fashion." He turned to Mish. "Isn't this so, Doctor?"

But the Doctor did not respond. He just sat there, staring into space.

"Dr. Mish," said Gemma, sitting next to him. "Yoo hoo, *Starbow* calling Dr. Mish!" She nudged him.

"There's danger," he breathed hoarsely. "Extreme danger!"

And then he fell over, face first, into Gemma Naquist's dessert.

Chapter Fourteen

It was an action spring-loaded with years of hate and fear, resentment and anxiety, orchestrated by the combat training given her by the Friends. For Laura Shemzak, all that had been bad in her life was focused on Overfriend Arnal Zarpfrin, architect of manipulation both subtle and overt. All she could feel was the triumphant surge of rage as she leaped over his desk, hands outstretched for his throat.

Zarpfrin was taken by surprise. Clearly, he had been so self-assured of the efficacy of his implant, his control of Laura, that he had taken no measures for personal safety against her other than the routine.

His expression only had time to register alarm before Laura was on him, her hands hitting his soft neck before he could bring up his arms in any kind of defense. The momentum of her force knocked him back, kicked his chair over.

They went down in a struggling heap, Laura managing to keep her hold while Zarpfrin's face grew red and his arms flailed.

Her vision focused only on him as she flung Zarpfrin's head back into the wall, once, twice, *bang! bang!* time seeming to stand still, only faintly aware of the voice in her head crying *Warning! Warning! Desist!*

All her life she had been a puppet, dangling from strings constructed by men like this, and this man was the worst of them, sending her out programmed to shoot Cal, then trying to make her betray her comrades.

He deserved to *die*!

This single driving thought kept her at him, kept her hanging on, kept back everything inside her that tried to tear her away.

Zarpfrin's face was turning a gratifying purple when the sound of thundering footsteps penetrated her berserk frenzy. A set of rough hands grabbed her, then another and another, as guards tried to tear her away from the Overfriend. Cursing and spitting, she used her cyborg strength and commando training to fling them off. It took them four tries until Laura was overcome by their sheer force of numbers. She found herself tumbling across the floor, crashing into a wall with an explosion of light and dark, gasping for air. She rolled to her feet, ready to fight, wanting only to kill, kill all of them.

"Don't try it, kid," said one of the security men. He had a power gun in his hand, aimed squarely at her chest. "Don't even think about it."

Automatically, she checked her intended leap.

Another security man was helping a bruised but still breathing Zarpfrin to his feet. "That . . . shouldn't have . . . happened. . . ." he said rubbing his throat where angry red marks from Laura's attack showed.

As Laura stood, wondering what to do next, the question was answered for her.

She screamed.

She clasped her hands against her head as though to tear out the unbearable agony that filled her as her anger and adrenaline faded away.

The implant *had* done its job.

It was leeching her Zernin's effects from her, and she was rapidly experiencing withdrawal.

Cold turkey.

She dropped to her knees, her face contorting into a rictus of pain. She felt as though her spine were being scoured by steel wool.

"I warned you, Laura," said Zarpfrin.

"What's wrong with her?" asked one of the security men.

"Should we get a doctor?"

"No. No, she'll live . . . but she won't like it much." He walked over to her. "Now, Laura, I'll forgive that little outburst. We all have tantrums once in a while. But I need to know where the *Starbow* is. Give me coordinates, Laura, and we'll let you sleep awhile. You'd like to sleep, wouldn't you, Laura?"

Laura nodded.

"Well, then, you know the information. Tell me."

She motioned to him and he bent closer.

She spit in his face.

One of the security men kicked her.

Zarpfrin stood up and took out a handkerchief, cleaning off the spittle. "Take her to one of the waiting rooms with no furniture," he said. "Lock her in for a while. Let her think this one over for about an hour. That will be enough. It will seem like an eternity to her in her present condition."

Two security men grabbed her arms and hauled her up.

"Don't worry, Laura," said Zarpfrin. "You won't die. You'll just wish you could."

They dragged her away, half conscious, whimpering.

Zarpfrin's last words to her were: "Remember, Laura. It doesn't have to be like this."

Laura barely heard him.

She was lying in a room.

On a rug.

She knew that much, though at times it seemed a very peculiar room, the walls twisting and cracking and pulsing like living things.

She hurt, but in ways beyond pain. Unimaginable ways she knew she could not bear, yet somehow managed to.

The room was bare of furniture. Strip lights were on the walls, shining dully down upon her torture.

The voice was gone, though any company would have been welcome, even that monotone nag.

The only thing that kept her going was thinking about the *Starbow*, thinking about Cal, thinking about Tars Northern, concentrating on them, knowing that she was doing the *good* thing, the *right* thing, the *necessary* thing.

But that didn't stop the torture. It never does, she supposed. And she wondered, Am I going to be able to take this, or will I break down?

And she honestly did not know.

Slowly, as the room slipped and slid beneath her and she felt the agony rip apart into hallucinations, she began to lose control. She could not take it. Her personality began to shred, and with it her resolve. She knew that if Zarpfrin walked in at that moment, she'd tell him the coordinates.

Tell him where the *Starbow* was.

Tell him, so this agony would end.

And if the agony *would* not end, perhaps she'd beg to be killed.

As she lay on the floor, feeling herself dissolve, she reached out toward something, anything: God, Nothingness, Eternity, Oblivion, and she prayed, PLEASE!

A voice fluttered in her head, "We hear . . ." and then was lost.

Nor was it the voice of the implant—that was gone now.

She restructured herself amidst her pain around that voice, and she called out again, reaching out with every muscle in her being.

"Who's . . . that?"

She began to see clouds swirling about her in multihues of color. A figure began to form. An older man, long of hair, bearded, with kindly eyes.

"I have been called Andrew," he said.

Andrew! Was this a figment of her tortured imagination? Andrew was one of the Aspach . . . Dr. Mish's brethren of the portals!

"Yes," said Andrew. "I am he. And you are Laura Shemzak, who has come to take us to safety."

"I'm not . . . doing much good, I'm afraid," she said. "I'm locked in a room, strung out on Zernin deprivation. . . . But how can we talk?"

"You have certain latent powers of the mind, psychic powers which you have, in your desperation, utilized."

"That doesn't do much good, I'm afraid," she said wearily. "I'm supposed to hustle you guys back within the circuitry of my blip-ship. But I'm a traitor, you see. I'm a weak fool. . . ."

"No, this is not true."

"They're going to get the information from me by hook or crook."

"Have faith, Laura Shemzak. There is a way."

"Tell me."

Silence for a moment. The figure flickered and wavered, losing focus for a moment, then returning.

"But there will be . . . a sacrifice that must be paid," said Andrew.

"What?"

"You must . . . surrender yourself to us. You must trust us totally."

"Continue," she said, still struggling to remain coherent.

"There is, in this room, an electrical outlet which interfaces with the Block computer. You must tap yourself into that outlet. You must allow yourself to become a vessel for us."

"Me? But how—"

"We knew you, Laura Shemzak. You are an XT pilot. Your cyborg implants, when powered by your auxiliary batteries, can form a complete electrical circuit . . . an environment in which we can survive."

"But . . . I'm a wreck!"

"Trust us, Laura. Trust us."

Somehow she managed to rise up out of her misty stupor. Although the pain and the need for Zernin were more acute here, she was able to have sensory contact with her surroundings. She saw the four sides of the room, the rug she lay on, the ceiling. There was a sour taste in her mouth and everything seemed rough and raw, as though scraped by a wood file.

She managed to prop herself up on her hands, focus her vision. . . .

Where was this outlet?

She rubbed her eyes and examined the walls as best she could again, trying to control her ragged breathing.

There it was!

It had a cover on it, the same gray color as the walls; that's why she hadn't seen it before. She dragged herself over to it, fighting back the dizziness and the pain, and she pulled open the cover.

It was a female plug, designed for insertion of a jack. She had nothing inside her that would work, and besides, her system surely wasn't compatible.

She let herself drop in a heap on the wall, wishing she was dead, letting the pain begin to claw her back into despair. . . .

"Laura," the voice of Andrew said. "There is a way . . . surrender . . . give yourself for those you love. . . ."

She opened her eyes.

Spread out before her were the fingers of her hand, and instantly she knew what she had to do.

Something in her rebelled against the notion, for it would hurt, but she had to almost laugh at that because she hurt anyway.

She took the forefinger of her left hand and began to worry the flesh at the tip with her teeth, biting down farther through plastic until the metal filament showed, then repeated this upon her middle finger.

She rested a moment, blood dripping on the rug.

It hadn't been too bad. Her hand had been designed

for tapping into computers; just not quite this way, that was all.

She lifted herself wearily and reached out again with her mind. *Does this mean I get to die?*

There was no answer.

Had it all be an illusion? Was the visitation of Andrew just the result of a tortured mind?

And the word came back to her. "Surrender . . ."

It went against all that she had fought for, but she said, "To hell with it," and jammed her finger prongs into the wall outlet.

The immediate surge of electricity almost forced her to black out. Smoke wisped up from her fingers, along with the smell of burnt blood and flesh.

And then she found her consciousness slipping away into interface with the computer . . . a familiar sensation, with the impression of power and logic matrix and macros and micros, except this time there was something more. . . .

Presences.

She could perceive the presence of intelligent beings, and they flowed into her with a clean, clear force.

Darkness snapped tight around her, but it was a welcome darkness for it brought peace and rest, and complete nothingness, like balm upon her soul.

When she woke up, she lay sprawled upon the floor, with the impression of only being away for a few minutes. There was a familiar *Who am I? Where am I?* quality to the experience; an inrush of newness, a cascade of tingling. . . .

She got up.

The room was the same, the rug was the same, the walls were the same.

But she wasn't the same.

She wasn't strung-out! She didn't hurt! If someone

had showed her a pinch of Zernin, she'd laugh in their face!

What the hell was going on here?

And then she remembered, and immediately she was aware of a throbbing in her fingers.

She pulled them up, examined them.

The blood had clotted. The imbedded prongs still stuck from her fingertips, shorn of flesh and plastic. So it hadn't been a nightmare.

But where . . . ?

"We're here, inside you, Laura Shemzak," said the voice she immediately identified as Andrew's. "Transference was successful."

Laura shivered at the thought. Possessed! Of course, lately that was nothing new!

"What have you done to me? I feel great! Physically, I mean."

"We made the necessary adjustments in your neurological and metabolic cyborg interface. You no longer need Zernin for everyday life."

"Thank you," she said. That was all she could think to say. "It made me . . . a traitor."

"Ultimately, you proved yourself stronger than it, Laura."

"Wait a minute. So now I've got you guys riding around in me . . . I'm still a prisoner! What good does that do any of us?"

"No good, unless we effect an escape."

"My middle name!"

"Good. You must somehow, of course, reach your blip-ship and pilot it back to the *Starbow*. There we can transfer to the energy field within which the one you call Mish survives."

"Yeah, a little more room than you've got now. I bet you've all got elbows in your eyes."

"Metaphorically, perhaps."

"But how do I get out? That's the question."

"Our reading of you reveals that you have remarkable powers of instantaneous choice based upon intuitive powers, a gift that has often removed you from difficulties."

"And often gotten me into trouble."

"Nonetheless, you must rely on it again."

"Right. Any help from you guys would be more than welcome."

"Naturally."

She went over and tried the door. It was locked.

"So I guess," she said, "I'm going to have to wait until they come and get me. It shouldn't be too long. Feels like I've already been in this place for ages."

"Not necessarily," said Andrew. "While you were asleep, we also took the liberty to adjust your cyborg components, with the necessity of escape in mind. If you will simply touch the lock with the contact points on your fingertips, we will do the rest."

"Oh."

Laura obeyed. A stream of electrical power crackled from her fingers. The lock snapped. The door opened.

"Wow," said Laura. "Great."

She stepped out into the drab hallway. No alarms were sounding. There were no guards to be seen, either.

"But which way?" Laura asked. And immediately the answer came to her, like a tremble of déjà vu. She struck out toward the right.

"Excellent, Laura," said Andrew. "A wonderful illustration of your talent. But you could have waited for the answer from us. We are quite aware of the direction you must go."

"Now you tell me."

"Take note that there is a guard posted around the next corner, Laura. We suggest that you render him unconscious and arm yourself with his hand weapon."

"Sure. If you'll give me that little hand-zap again!"

"With pleasure!"

Sure enough, there he was, stationed right outside an elevator. Short and handsome, in a brutish Feddy way.

Laura instantly knew that stealth was not the way to handle this particular occasion. She walked directly up to the guard, practically bumping into him with her chest. "Hi! Can you tell me which way it is to the ladies room?"

Her hand shot out. A small bit of electricity hit him just behind his ear. He went down like a sack of potatoes.

"Jeez, you didn't kill him, did you?" asked Laura.

"No. A simple stunning. Visually impressive, perhaps, but no harm will come to him."

"I really don't care, but it just seemed unnecessary."

"Our thoughts precisely."

She kneeled by him, took his power pistol from him. "Elevator, right?"

"That is correct."

"Lobby."

"A very direct method."

"The fastest, and I don't think they're expecting this."

"No, that is absolutely true."

She took the elevator.

The vital factor, of course, was time. How much longer did she have before Zarpfrin decided she had suffered enough and sent those guards back to shovel up the pieces and deposit her back in his office, to try again to get the location of the *Starbow*? She could almost visualize his face when he discovered she was gone. She smiled wryly at the thought.

The doors opened upon nothing much exciting in the lobby: the usual checkpoints, strolling people, air of deadness.

She walked casually down the corridor toward the access tube to the small Block starport, ready at any time to go for the pistol tucked into her belt. Her senses were clear and alert, and she felt keen and alive, even without the Zernin coursing through her veins.

She took the tube car to the starport terminal, then walked to the security checkpoint. "Hello," she said, extending her good hand for identification check. "I'm Laura Shemzak. I just got here this morning. Checked into Berth 1943. I'm checking out now. My business with Overfriend Zarpfrin has been completed."

The man behind the desk wore a professional frown as he reviewed his screen. He looked up, his frown somehow deeper. "I'm sorry, Pilot Shemzak, but I've received no release procedures for you from the proper authorities. If you'll wait a moment, I'll see what I can do."

"Oh! Of course! I forgot the release Overfriend Zarpfrin gave me." She reached to her belt, drew out the gun quickly, and stunned the man into unconsciousness. "There!"

She didn't wait for a car to take her out onto the field, but found the nearest exit and headed toward her blipship on foot.

The sky was bright with a spatter of clouds, and a nice breeze tousled her hair as she ran. She was halfway to her docking berth before the alarms began to ring.

"What now?" she said.

"Run!" said Andrew.

"What a brilliant suggestion!"

Fortunately, she had only about another two hundred yards to go. Thank God she had a small ship with antigrav; if it was larger, it would have had to be docked on the other side of the field, away from things.

She ran at top speed and was surprised at what good shape she was in, despite her recent exhausting bout with Zernin withdrawal.

The ship was up ahead, unguarded. It looked good— sleek salvation. She yearned to jam the attachments inside her, feel the power course through her, the rockets blowing, the suspensers pushing her up toward the haven of space, away from this dreadful world.

She was almost there when she heard shouts behind her: "Halt! Stop!"

And the pound of pursuing feet.

Damn!

But there was still time. She stamped up the access ladder, punched out the code on the hull. The door opened, and she jumped into the small compartment.

A low-intensity volley of energy weapons smashed against the hull. She slammed the door closed and immediately went into linking procedure, hitting the warm-up toggle. The XT 9 began to thrum and buck in its berth like an anxious, feisty bronco sensing imminent release. She plugged herself in, and started mentally directing the next actions.

But nothing more happened.

Her consciousness did not expand to become the blip-ship, nor would the thing obey her commands.

"What the hell—" she said, for there was nothing restraining the ship. And then she knew.

The Zernin.

She must be out of Zernin, and somehow that drug had been able to allow the intimate link with her nervous system, her cyborg components, her mind, and the XT 9.

And there were no manual controls on a blip-ship.

She could hear the power beams hitting the hull as she sat, shocked.

She was trapped!

Chapter Fifteen

"*This* is Omega Space?" said Ratham Bey, turning around and surveying the strange landscape. "*This* is what we've been knocking our brains out for?"

"You and the Jaxdron," Cal returned mildly. "And who knows who else?"

"But it's just some kind of plain on a planet." He sipped his drink. "A plain with mountains in the distance and a weird sky. I mean, this seems to be just a point in normal space!"

"At first," said Cal, pacing leisurely. "But then you notice that it's different here . . . or more precisely, it's *more* like normal space . . . certain aspects of normal space."

"Where'd you get this drink? And this chair." The dark-skinned man's eyes shone very brown as wonder sank into them.

"Yes, and that's part of the point," said Cal. "But let's get some real world facts straight first. I'll go first."

He gave Bey a brief rundown on how he had been captured by the Jaxdron, how they had put him through all sorts of tests, shuttled him hither and thither, and finally perfected the group of clones to be linked in the mind matrix to augment his own intelligence and powers and thus form a portal to this plane of existence.

"But I outfoxed them, you see. I jumped through, closed the portal, and escaped. Only what I'm going to do now that I've escaped, I really can't say. But then, this is a hell of a lot better than being held prisoner by a bunch of crazy aliens."

Bey nodded. "Incredible. But how do you know they won't be able to figure out a way to reopen the rift?"

"Unlikely. That's why they needed me, you see . . . and now they don't have me!"

He folded his arms with satisfaction. "But I should sit down, too, I suppose."

He visualized a plushly cushioned, high-backed chair. It was suddenly there before him, red and comfy-looking. He sat down and looked at Ratham Bey.

"Amazing," said Bey.

Cal shrugged. "You just have to know how to do it. I'll explain later. Right now, I'd like to hear about the *Starbow* and how you got here yourself."

"Well, I'm only an officer aboard the *Starbow*—a lieutenant. I was recruited in the Pleiades sector—after what the Federation did to my planet, I was ready for vengeance, let me tell you. But you don't want to hear about me, you want to hear about Laura Shemzak."

"She's with you? God, I wondered why you were looking for me and not the damned Feddies! How is she?"

"She's a handful, your sister is."

Cal grinned. "Oh, yes, she is! I don't know many other people who would try to move the starways to perform an impossible rescue."

"It wasn't easy for her, I'll say that!"

Bey related the events that had occurred from Laura's arrival on board the *Starbow* after its attack on the *Ezekiel*, including the retrieval of the XT 9 on Short-child, Laura's rescue of Captain Tars Northern, and their journey to Baleful, the class L planet in the Cori-dian sector.

"Wait a minute," said Cal. "How did you know I was there?"

"We didn't, but Laura did. Federation analysis beams read the retreat of the Jaxdron ships that at-tacked Mulliphen sufficiently long to calculate high probability they were taking you there. It was a planet previously controlled by the Federation, now owned by the Jaxdron. It made sense.''

"Right. They needed me on the Fault. Okay. But I didn't stay there long. For some reason they shipped me off again. Maybe because they had better facilities on another base, who knows? But what happened?''

"We got an SOS from one of the atmosphere domes. We figured it was you, trying to contact any possible rescue attempt. Needless to say, it wasn't you. But they left behind three of those cyborg clones of you.''

"No kidding.''

"Yes. And Laura shot one of them dead.''

Cal went white. "She *what*?''

"Yes, she didn't care much for that either.''

"Did it attack her?''

"No. Overfriend Zarpfrin had placed an implant on her optical nerve.''

"He wanted me dead! Of course! He didn't want the Jaxdron to use me to get into Omega Space!''

"Something like that, apparently. Anyway, Laura was understandably relieved when she found out that it wasn't really you she had blasted.''

"Nice to know.''

"We had a scrape with the Jaxdron, and some sort of broadcast from them that we'd find you—and our destiny—on Snar'shill.''

"So that's where I was!''

"It's almost as though the Jaxdron were toying with us. As though it were all some vast game!''

"You hit the nail on the head there, pal,'' said Cal. "That's exactly where their heads are at.''

"Pardon?''

"From the very beginning I was forced to run through all sorts of games. Their way of testing me, I thought. But it was more than that. I spoke to them. That's the way they see things—as some sort of cosmic game to which only they know the rules.''

"Curious.''

"You bet. A mystery and an enigma too! But that's just something we'll have to solve later. So tell me more. How did you get here?''

"Oh, that's an entirely different, though related, story. You see, we've got this alien on board the ship, name of Shontill.''

Ratham Bey explained to Cal about Shontill and his search for his lost race, the Frin'ral. He told of the discovery of the Frin'ral derelict ship. . . .

"There was some sort of portal inside. And quite simply, I got sucked in. The rest was just like limbo . . . until somehow you conjured me back into existence. Thank you, by the way.''

"My pleasure,'' said Cal thoughtfully. "They're still hot on my tail, then, bent upon rescuing me?''

"Yes, and getting into Omega Space as well.''

"Encouraging.''

Ratham Bey finished his drink. "I don't know how much time has passed, but please, I'm no scientist, just a pretty good ship's gunner and navy man.'' He gestured around. "What is this place?''

"Think about it. Omega Space . . . as opposed to Alpha Space.''

"Our dimension.''

"Right. Beginning and end. Interconnected yet different. Now, I won't go into the quantum mechanics—the physics involved—I'll simply put things into simple, laymen's terms. They don't make sense any other way.''

"I'm listening.''

"The average intelligent being is trained to think about their existence in a certain way by the culture they are born in. They are taught reality, but it's a construct reality, created by the society and culture purely for self-continuation. But anyone with imagination breaks out of those reality chains, sees things differently, makes things different. But then, after this breakthrough, whether it be personal or technological or philosophical, the mechanics of culture assume it . . . and it becomes part of the status quo.

"Human beings operate under certain assumed laws in our universe. It's very objective. But when you get down to the basic structure of existence, you see that the universe cannot exist without you to participate in its existence. Thus, we create our own universe, create our own boundaries and limitations . . . and well we should, because otherwise, chances are there'd be no laws and parameters, nothing to compare things with, no sense whatever.

"Omega Space is simply a full expression of this aspect of existence, a place where literally anything can happen, as long as you know how to make it happen, as long as you know that it's your mind that is creating everything all the time. In a very real way, the reason it looks like this right now, this plain, these mountains, is because that's apparently the way that I want it to be . . . subconsciously, perhaps, but all the same . . . it's something that my conscious mind can understand, assimilate, deal with easily. But say I want a house, or a chair, or another glass of iced tea for you—I can change the fabric to create it, right out of nothing. Because that's the truth about Omega Space—it's the intersection between absolute nothingness and something. The plane of creation itself."

"No wonder the Jaxdron want it."

"But you say that the Frin'ral are here . . . they escaped here, somehow."

"Correct. The question is, where are they? If it's nothingness, then they're nowhere."

"But if they know the nature of Omega Space sufficiently, then they're everywhere they care to be."

"Look," said Ratham Bey. "These philosophical answers are all very well and good. And it's nice to know that we won't starve or go thirsty and we can sit down on comfortable chairs. But how do we get out of here?''

"Good question. Maybe the Frin'ral know. We'll have to try and find them.''

"So where do we look?''

"Tell me more about this Shontill fellow. What does he look like, how does he act, that sort of thing. Give me an idea of who the creature is.''

Ratham Bey shrugged. "Sure. I'll do the best I can.''
The man described Shontill.''

"Big, huh?''

"Yes.''

"Fierce?''

"I guess sometimes . . . but might merely be the way you would interpret him from a human perspective.''

"Good enough. Thanks, Ratham. Now what I want you to do is to close your eyes and visualize Shontill . . . or rather, creatures like Shontill. I want you to see them here, now . . . and I want you to imagine them talking to us.''

"Okay, I understand. Sort of the way you brought me here.''

"Precisely.''

Cal Shemzak did not close his own eyes. Instead, he picked out a spot ahead of them both, and thought about Shontill the way Lieutenant Bey had described him—the stature, the broad shoulders, the roughly humanoid face, the tentacles turning into arms. He doubled this image, tripled it . . .

And three members of the Frin'ral race stood before them.

They spoke in a guttural alien tongue.

"Good grief,'' said Ratham Bey, opening his eyes. "It worked!''

"Hold a moment,'' said Cal. "We need something else.''

He visualized the necessary object in his hand. It appeared: a translator.

"This is not necessary," said one of the Frin'ral. "We have already read your minds, and know your tongue."

"Then you know who we are as well," said Cal.

"Yes."

"Can you help us?"

"You must come with us to our home. The home of our people. Then we will see in what way we can help you."

Bey said, "Is it a long walk?"

"We need not walk," said another of the Frin'ral. "We shall bring it here."

And in an instant they were surround by buildings of quite peculiar architecture—tilted, leaning, towering.

"Toto," said Cal Shemzak, "I don't think we're in Kansas anymore."

Chapter Sixteen

"I can't do it!" Pilot Shemzak wailed. "I can't make frakking contact!"

It was one of her worst nightmares. She sat there, in the snug cockpit of her XT 9, her blip-ship, and she felt useless, impotent, and exhausted.

She was no good. She had failed. She had failed the *Starbow*, failed Tars Northern, failed these beings within her, failed Cal, and ultimately failed herself.

Tears sprang helplessly to her eyes.

She could hear the power beams from the soldiers outside, raking against the force-field around the hull, and she knew it wouldn't be long.

"O ye of little faith," said Andrew inside her.

"I can't do it!" said Laura. "I just don't have the power, the ability without that damned drug."

"Relax," said the voice. "I shall stay within you while my brethren take up residence in the circuitry of the vessel. Watch!"

Even as the voice spoke, Laura could see that her whole body was beginning to glow with a soft nimbus. Her wires and attachments glittered for a moment; there was the sound of moving air, a vibrant *Whoosh!* a tinkling kind of sound . . .

The whole interior sparkled like diamonds lit from within.

And Laura could feel power beginning to flow through her and from her; she could feel her mind opening up like a flower, its petals reaching into every nook and cranny of the blip-ship. It was like usual, with the drug *zing*ing through her synapses, effervescent and alive, only *cleaner*. She was amazed.

"I suggest you take off now, Pilot Shemzak," said Andrew.

"Oh, yeah. Good idea."

Laura reached, flexed the engines, the suspensers, and she was off, springing up from the landing pad effortlessly, feeling shiny and new in the late afternoon sun.

She automatically stepped up the force-fields to allow for any random shots from below. She opened her sensor pods wide for indications of pursuit, adjusted her personal-grav. She took a roll and a bank for evasive action, then blasted off through the atmosphere.

"Hot damn!" she screeched, feeling alive again. "Awesome!"

She lost herself in the thrill, the racing ecstasy of rising up through the atmosphere, through the friction, like rising from a pool of water to finally break out in a burst of spray at the surface. But up in the ionosphere her alarms rang, sensors indicating that she was being pursued from the surface.

"Got a healthy start on them!" she whooped, racing out toward where the shadowed moon hung, then veering out of ecliptic. The thing was, it would be stupid to shoot out through where all the Federation forces were—much simpler to rise up above that plane, gain some distance from the gravity wells, and hit the jump motors. And they didn't know where the hell the *Starbow* was.

But her joy was stillborn. Coming out of nowhere, two sleek Federation cruisers—heavy-duty cruisers, new ones, bristling with weapons and coursing with energy—erupted into position just a couple hundred kilometers behind her tail.

What the hell!

She pushed up her acceleration another half-G, starting to feel it despite her grav-control, but still her sensors showed the Fed cruisers gaining on her.

Damn! She had at least fifteen minutes to go at top acceleration before she could even think about tripping out into her Underspace jump!

Each second that ticked off, the ships were closer to her.

"Hey, Andrew, can you get me out of this one?"

There was no response.

Presumably the being was concentrating on the problem as much as she, milking every last bit of power from the XT 9.

The star field glittered ahead, cold and dead and barren again, reflecting the fear and doubt that was growing malignantly inside her.

Then she began picking up attempted communication on a message frequency. She opened up her audio and listened: "Shemzak, pilot of XT 9, you will commence deceleration immediately. Prepare for surrender. Any escape is impossible. We outpower you."

"Suck meteorites, Fed-head," Laura blasted back. "I'll surrender to death before I surrender to you."

"That, Pilot Shemzak, is your only alternative."

Desperately, Laura checked her readings again to ascertain the possibility of a premature jump. No way. No frakking way! If I jump now, she thought, the only stuff that will come out on the other side of Underspace will be puree.

She willed the blip-ship to go faster, but with no luck. The cruisers were gaining on her kilometer by kilometer. It wouldn't be long before they'd be within sufficient range to blast her with their heavy artillery.

"Andrew . . . you guys know any more magic tricks?" she asked.

Andrew, however, did not answer; still she felt his presence.

"I'll just assume that you're working on the problem," she said.

The deep-space radio crackled again.

"Laura. This is Zarpfrin." Smooth, almost friendly tones. "Why are you doing this?"

He must be talking on a channel from Earth, she realized.

"Pretty surprised, huh, Zarpy?" she shot back. "Thought you had me. You're just too damned self-confident for your own good! Now what is the Council going to say . . . especially about all that awful chicanery you've been up to!"

"I am in full cooperation with the Council, Laura Shemzak," responded the radio voice immediately. "But this is not the matter we must discuss. Captains Karn and Dano of the cruisers rapidly gaining on you tell me that it is merely a matter of three minutes before their power beams can easily pick you out of space. So it's a matter of your life, Laura Shemzak. At this point, should you continue to flee, no attempt will be made to apprehend you. We'll simply destroy you. It's that simple. So I implore you to surrender immediately."

"So you can shoot me full of drugs again? So you can twist my head out of shape, control me, manipulate me? Uh-uh, Zarpfrin, no go. I'd rather die. But I'll die with a smile on my face, knowing how much it's gonna spite you!"

Silence.

"Very well, Laura, if that is your choice," said Zarpfrin, his voice detectably shaky. "Good-bye."

The transmission was cut off.

The seconds ticked away, slowing down to a numbing crawl as the XT 9 strained desperately toward the stars.

"C'mon, boat," Laura said through clenched teeth. "Just a little more. Please!"

She checked out her sensors. The weapons blisters on the cruisers were hot and ready. Doubtless even now they were being aimed at her—her tiny ship in Feddy crosshairs, itchy fingers on the triggers, waiting for the order to fire.

She perceived the glow of building energy at the tips

of the blisters, signaling the imminence of fire.

And at the last moment she banked, and swerved downward.

The energy beams converged in the space where she had been.

She began further evasive action, again avoiding a hit, but losing distance in the process, making her more of a target.

She was just buying time, she knew, waiting for something to happen. A miracle, perhaps. Yeah, that would be what she needed right now—an outright miracle.

What she got instead was the swipe of an energy beam.

It hit her near the tail; if not for her protective force-field, it would have blown her away. As it was, it merely did a great deal of damage and sent her off on a wild tangent, spinning crazily.

She was out of control.

Still, the hit gave her more time, as the cruisers had to plot her erratic course. Bet they couldn't guess this one, she thought with morbid glee.

But it killed half her propulsive force. Within seconds, she'd be a goner.

Wait a minute, she thought, her mind suddenly clear again. I'm using the wrong mentality here.

Although she couldn't escape, her mobility rockets and beams were still effective. She fought for the helm of her ship. She got it back. Without further thought she went crazy, veering her course abruptly so that she was headed straight at the ships.

She picked the closest, and stitched a series of damaging shots across its bow, blowing away the weapons placements there.

She laughed crazily, feeling in control. If she was going to go out, she would go out in bright lights and style!

The other cruiser tried to track her.

She had an idea. A vicious idea. She let herself slow

down, become a target, keeping herself on the weapon-less side of the cruiser she had attacked. She sensed the energy nodes approaching fire, and immediately shot away.

Instead of hitting her, the beams smacked into the side of the sister cruiser, blowing a wide hole.

Laura giggled, and headed straight for the other one, able to avoid the beams at this close range, dealing the cruiser a couple of blows before zipping away in the opposite direction.

Let's see them veer around! she thought.

Of course, she was now headed back in the direction in which she had come, which was not a good idea, but it gave her time to think.

Or she thought it would.

Instead, as her sensors automatically felt out the space beyond her, they detected certain unwelcome company. A whole fleet's worth of Federation ships, coming from several directions, heading straight for her!

Uh-oh! No way she was going to slip through that crew!

"Andrew," she said sadly. "I'll do my best, but I think that we've bought the farm."

Again, no response.

Still, she was yet one with her ship, so the Aspach were still there.

But what the hell were they doing?

She spun about and tried for a run, but it was thoroughly ridiculous: her engines sounded like they had a terminal case of whooping cough. Inside the ship, even in her contact/trance state, she could hear them rattling spastically.

She felt oddly detached—the panorama of space, the stars, the Earth, the Moon, surrounding her coldly, like a tomb this time, an eternal sepulcher. No longer did it mean freedom for her. No, as she always expected it would be, she was going to die in the forever quiet of space.

And she was curiously calm about that fact; amazingly at peace.

She was her own person. She hadn't sold out the ones she loved, had not betrayed them. This was a good time to die.

Her sensors read that it was only a minute or two before this fleet of Federation ships surrounded her. She stopped expending her energy on the useless attempt at escape. She would need all her power to let them have it with her particle beam weapons, so that they couldn't lock a tractor beam on her; they'd have to blow her out of the sky in mere self-defense.

They came closer, closer, visible dots growing into tremendous islands of metal moving in space.

She turned on her radio, open frequency, and she said something very rude, just so these guys would never forget her. And she got ready to blast.

But then something strange happened.

Just a few hundred meters off her starboard side, something began to materialize.

Just a shimmer at first, a wavering of the stars—and then suddenly it was there, in an explosion of dazzling light.

It was a spaceship.

It had a long, sleek body, with spokes radiating from this hub. At the end of each of these spokes were jewel-like appendages. They sparkled and pulsed with energy.

They'd never done that before, was Laura Shemzak's first thought. And then it sank in.

The starship was the *Starbow*.

They'd come for her.

"What are you idiots doing here?" she demanded over the radio. "You're gonna get yourselves decimated."

Captain Northern's voice erupted over the radio line.

"Would you shut your mouth and get your ass inside! Docking bay is open . . . now!"

She didn't waste any time. Rocketing forward, she steadied herself with the necessary beams, and then, the moment she had enough room to pass through the unfolding doors, she zoomed up and into the belly of the ship, docking.

"Good show, Laura. You got your cargo?"

"That's right."

"Do a quick computer check hookup. The Aspach will be able to use the connection to flow into the large circuitry."

"Gotcha."

Even as the docking doors were closing and the bay repressurized, she maneuvered the necessary device to lock into the computer interface in her berth. It slipped in and she opened contact.

"Bye, guys. Hope you liked the ride." She felt a draining effect as they departed. And she heard Andrew say, "You have done well, Laura. We leave you adjusted, so that you will be free. But you will not be able to fly this vessel."

"Thanks. That's okay. It's busted, anyway." Laura felt Andrew depart. She could detect the familiar folding-in of her consciousness as it withdrew from the circuits of the XT 9. But otherwise she felt no depression, no physical letdown of reduced Zernin and adrenaline. Andrew's praise warmed her, and she felt the satisfaction of a job well done. When atmosphere was returned to the docking bay, Laura opened the hatch and stepped out.

She took a look at her ship and saw that it was just as bad as she thought.

She sighed and gave the vessel a mock salute. "It's been fun, pal. But so long!"

Then she spun on her heel and raced up toward the bridge to see how the hell Northern and Mish were gonna get their tails out of this crack!

Chapter Seventeen

When Laura raced through the door and onto the bridge, she immediately noticed two things: the tension was so thick you could cut it with a proverbial knife. And the viewscreens were filled with Federation battleships, getting larger and larger as they got nearer and nearer.

It stopped Laura dead.

"What's the phrase?" she asked. "Out of the frying pan, into the fire?"

The crew were all in battle stations. Red lights flashed. Voices were terse; even the computer voices, it seemed. A few eyes flashed Laura's way, noted her presence, then turned back to work. Dr. Mish slouched limply in his chair, in some kind of trance.

Captain Tars Northern stood up from his command chair, his face clearly aglow at seeing Laura. He stepped over to her, and she grabbed him and held him hard. Softly she said, "Thank you. Thank you so much, Tars."

He held her away from him, making sure all of her was there. "Did you bring the supercargo?"

"Yes. Apparently they made the transfer just fine. They saved me, Tars. They saved me from myself."

"Good. Mish is busy figuring out the next step. And it's got to be pretty damned fast too. Our shields aren't going to be able to hold out against that kind of firepower for very long."

"Mish . . . yes. Tars, those spokes . . . the ends . . . it was almost magical. And you're not supposed to be able to jump into a system like this!"

"One of the *Starbow*'s little secrets, but we only do it

in emergencies. Takes up an incredible amount of energy, and damned chancy to boot! I guess right now he's greeting his pals. Hopefully he's working on getting us out of this mess."

"If you came here using that method, why can't you leave that way as well?"

"Power supply is too low," Tars said.

"How did you know to come for me?"

"Little message transmission from the Aspach. Apparently they were close enough for some kind of contact, and Mish pretty much knew what was going on."

"Then you know. . . ."

Tars nodded solemnly, and squeezed her shoulder comfortingly. "Yes, Laura, we know all about it. But look, you've done your bit. What I want you to do now is to just go over to the empty chair and tie yourself in. This place is going to be jumping pretty hard . . . and soon, I'll wager."

"Captain," said Tether Mayz, looking up from the blinking communications board. "We've got a message coming in from those Federation ships."

"Wonderful. We'll have a chance to buy some time. Open up the channel on the intercom, Tether."

A kind of hiss dropped from the speakers inlaid in the walls; a crackling became a voice.

". . . I repeat, this is Overfriend Arnal Zarpfrin of the Federation, speaking from Federation Headquarters on Earth. *Starbow*, do you read me?"

"We read you loud and clear, Zarpfrin."

He looked around at the assembled crew at their stations, and winked. Laura, hooking herself into place in a seat to the rear, knew that the captain was pleased: the transmission time between messages to and from the surface of Earth would make the conversation longer and thus buy them more time.

"Excellent," came Zarpfrin's voice finally. "I don't know where you came from, Northern, or how you did it, all I know is that my captains out there have got you completely surrounded. Now, I could simply order them to let loose with their weapons and transform you, your crew, and the *Starbow* into random bits of energy. On the other hand, if you surrender and allow a boarding party to come and take you away, I promise you a fair trial. And the possibility of new lives for you all. Doesn't seem to be much of a choice, does it, Captain?''

''What you seem to be trying to say, Zarpfrin, is: Surrender or die!''

Seconds passed.

Laura glanced over at Mish—no sign of animation at all.

She could see on the viewscreen that dozens of Federation ships surrounded them, their energy weapons sparkling with held-back energy, just waiting for the order to send it hurtling at the *Starbow*.

''That's right, Captain. So what is your answer going to be? I'll give you exactly one minute, plus transmission time, to answer.''

Northern glanced at his watch, and smiled grimly.

He motioned Tether Mayz to close the channel. Then he looked at the crew.

''Unfortunately we can't rely on Mish right now . . . but we can give him every bit of time he needs to do what he can. So this is the plan. If I tell Zarpfrin to go to hell, we immediately get blasted. But if I surrender, it will take some time for the boarding party to arrive . . . and time, needless to say, is a precious commodity at this point.'' He smiled.

Heads bobbed in agreement. It was a good plan.

Northern let the seconds tick away to the deadline, then motioned to Officer Mayz, who opened the line again.

''Zarpfrin, I think you're scum, and I hate what you Feddies stand for. But I can't justify the death of all my crew. As captain of the *Starbow*, I surrender to you. I can only hope that some of my crew will come out of this ordeal alive. Send a boarding party if you like. We'll cooperate fully." Northern paused. "You sonofa-bitch, you won!" His voice cracked, and he stifled a sob. Ending the transmission, he smiled up at his crew. "Pretty good, huh?"

"Excellent, Captain," Zarpfrin replied. "You are much wiser than I thought. Now, I will give the line over to Captain Follet of the *Andromeda*, who will give you the specifics of what will be required of you. And Tars . . . I look forward to seeing both you and Chivon again. I hope that the meeting will, this time, be much more pleasant."

"I can hardly wait," said Northern.

Captain Follet came on the line and identified himself. "As a further signal of your cooperation, Captain Northern, I want you to turn off your protective shielding."

Northern shrugged. "Certainly. Mr. Thur, would you please turn off primary, secondary, and tertiary force-screens."

Fingers stiff with tension went to work. The shields flipped off one by one.

"Now I want you to open your docking bay. We'll be sending two shuttles. One with a team of specialists who will take over the operation of the *Starbow* forthwith. The other will carry you and your crewmates back to the *Andromeda*, where you will be incarcerated for the duration, until you can be shipped back to Earth. Is that understood, Captain?'

"Perfectly."

"I want you to keep this channel open. Remain in constant contact with us. Any sign of the slightest at-tempt to resist us, and the large array of weapons now trained on your ship will be triggered."

"Understood," said Captain Northern, his eyes growing a little nervous as they flicked to Mish, still unmoving in his chair.

The minutes passed slowly, until finally the viewscreen showed the shuttles heading their way, growing from mere pinpricks of light into fairly large vessels.

"I'm afraid we're going to have to open the docking bay doors now," said Captain Northern wearily. "Can't stall any longer."

"Aye, aye, sir," said Gemma Naquist, performing the operation.

Northern stepped over to the limp body of Dr. Mish. "Come on, old fellow!" he said urgently. "We're counting on you to come through for us . . . or you're going to be just as lost as we are!"

There was no response.

"Captain, the first shuttle is about to reach the docking bay," reported one of the officers.

Northern turned away in exasperation from Dr. Mish's body. "Damn! There must be something we can do to stall them longer!"

"Captain!" said Navigator Dansen Jitt tremulously. "Look. Look at Mish!"

Laura turned and looked even as the captain twirled around.

Mish's hand was starting to glow!

"Mish!" said Captain Northern. "Mish, what do we do?"

Dr. Mish did not respond. The light, however, started to rapidly course up his arm, streaming into his face, spreading a scintillating cover over the entire area.

Then, quite suddenly, Laura realized that she was glowing as well, just as she had when she had let the Aspach pour through her.

They all began to twinkle.

"What the hell is going on?" came a shout.

And then everything shifted. The viewscreens, the lights, everything went completely dark for one moment. . . .

Then came back on.

Only this time, the viewscreen held no sign of the fleet

of Federation ships. There was only star-spotted space in front of them, in back of them, above them.

Arkm Thur whooped. "We did it! We jumped back to our previous coordinates."

Silver Zenyo seemed more surprised at what showed on her instruments. "Captain! We've somehow picked up a full complement of energy! We can head back into Underspace at any time, sir."

Northern knelt beside Mish's body. "Good show, old fellow! Can you come out and talk to us now?"

Dr. Mish's eyes opened. He looked around and smiled broadly. "I am complete," he said simply.

He turned around to Laura, who was just detaching herself from her seat. "I have much to thank you for, Pilot Shemzak. My brethren are reunited with me . . . and I am more able to function in aspects of my true capacity."

"You know about the Zernin, though," Laura said, hanging her head.

"Yes," said Dr. Mish. "The task was harder for you than we realized it would be. But your sacrifice and your bravery will long be remembered and cherished."

"I should be the one thanking you," said Laura. "You and your fellows, I mean. I'm clean now. I don't need the stuff anymore. Of course I can't fly a blip-ship —but it's a small price to pay, really."

Still, she felt a bit empty, a bit haunted now that the excitement of escape was waning. For years, her life had centered around her role as an XT pilot.

Tars Northern seemed to read that emptiness. He stepped over to her. Wrapping his arm around her he said, "You'll always be a pilot, Laura. As a matter of fact," he continued cheerily, "it just so happens that we could use another master pilot, couldn't we, people?"

The crew assented.

"And so, Lieutenant Laura Shemzak," Northern smiled, "you will receive the necessary instruction as soon as possible."

"Lieutenant?" Laura said. "You're making me a Lieutenant? But how—"

"Oh, I assure you, all rankings on the *Starbow* are pretty much arbitrary." There was mischief gleaming in the captain's eye. "Just for fun. For example, at a whim I can make myself *Admiral* Northern. After all, we're really not military, we're just starhounds."

"Pardon me, Admiral," said First Mate Arkm Thur. "I think it would really be advisable to resume our Underspace journey. I'm going to need a destination."

"Make it our previous destination, Mr. Thur."

"That would be Snar'shill, in the Dominus Cluster."

"Absolutely correct." He winked at Laura. "We're going to get Calspar Shemzak, and Overfriend Arnal Zarpfrin be damned!"

Chapter Eighteen

Overfriend Arnal Zarpfrin sat before the Council of Five, awaiting their decision as to his political future.

None of the Council were smiling.

Wreaths of cigarette smoke twisted up from the pinched countenance of Overfriend Visto. "You are the most recent of our number, Arnal Zarpfrin," he began, "and the most active and mobile. You had our approval on a number of projects and plans . . . and yet from all the evidence that we've been accumulating," he gestured back at ghostly documents hanging in the air, "it would seem that you have been involved in actions we have not been aware of."

"Nor would we have approved them," Overfriend Mazerk said, leaning toward him, fixing her sharp gray eyes on Zarpfrin.

"Just what is going on?" Overfriend Banili demanded imperiously.

Overfriend Zarpfrin smiled. "I've been a very bad boy, my friends, but all in a very good cause, I assure you!" He smiled all around, even at the two guards standing on either side of him, holding power guns at the ready. "Everything I've done, I've done for the sake of the Federated Empire!"

"Secret contact with the Jaxdron . . . for the sake of the Federation? A treasonous alliance with an alien enemy?" exclaimed Overfriend Fernk. "Subversive spying action involving a Federation Corporation . . . there's a whole laundry list of charges against you, Zarpfrin! We're just beginning to understand what you've been up to! Your obsessions, your ambitions, are wholly out of place in what, after all, is a cooperative arrangement by we administrators of a sacred trust!" Overfriend Fernk's mouth twitched nervously. He ran a hand through his short, grizzled hair. "This affair with Pilot Laura Shemzak and Friend Chivon Lasster . . . wholly beyond the pale! We have a number of facts before us. We would like you to tie them all together for us . . . before we make our decision as to your fate."

Overfriend Zarpfrin nodded. "Fair enough. Although the ramifications are complex, the beginnings are simple enough. And I trust you'll understand why I had to keep all of this to myself." He took a sip of tea, then looked around at the assembly. "Five years ago we made contact with the Jaxdron. I was in charge of extraterrestrial contact at that time. As you may recall, the Jaxdron quite easily took over a few of our outlying planets. They sparred with our fleets. We even seemed to beat them once. But then the *Excelsior* was taken captive by the Jaxdron. A month later it was returned, crew quite unharmed, with its captain, one Giles Raken, a spokesman for the Jaxdron."

"We have no record of this!" said Overfriend Visto.

"Of course not. I thought it best to keep it a secret, for reasons you will soon understand," continued Zarpfrin. "The message that Captain Raken brought was quite remarkable. Essentially, the Jaxdron were pleased to discover us and had no large territorial demands, nor did they desire the extermination of the human race, whom they found quite interesting."

"Whatever did they want then?" demanded Mazerk.

"They wanted to . . . play with us!"

There was a stunned silence in the group.

Zarpfrin paused for dramatic effect then continued. "Yes . . . a markedly superior group, the Jaxdron—better ships, better weapons—they could have taken over

half our worlds by this time, with sufficient armies to
control them. But no, they wanted to play. They wanted
to continue to have the odd battle, the odd planetary
takeover, but with fairly even match-ups. If this was
reasonable to our leaders, then the deal would be this:
do not notify your fleets that this is all just play, just
strange exercises on their parts . . . act as though it's for
real and no serious threat will be posed to the bulk of
your worlds!''

"Outrageous!''

"Ghastly!''

"Preposterous!''

"Well, that was my response at first as well, but then
I considered, and it sounded interesting and not that in-
sane, really. Naturally, we know from our experience
with the AI project that there are indeed conquering
races out in the galaxies. But why did they all have to be
that way? I mean, I am the very first to admit to a
paranoia on the subject. This, after all, is the reason I
called for all of those alien ships to be destroyed. We
need time, gentles, time to develop and to grow scien-
tifically and technologically.

"I said yes to the Jaxdron. Yes, we'll play . . . and
we'll continue this 'war' . . . and I kept this knowledge
to myself and my immediate associates for two reasons.

"The first reason, gentles, is quite obvious. All of you
know it because I was the one who proposed the plan in
the first place. The Jaxdron terrorize the Free Worlds,
Free Worlds come to the Federation for protection, we
provide the 'protection' . . . and it's all just a ploy to get
our ships within range of the planet, infiltrate the military structure, foment rebellion, and then force reunion
with the Federation.

"The second reason is more subtle. A culture at war
invariably develops faster in scientific and technological
ways. This 'play' war with the Jaxdron—with the society not realizing it was just play—would send us zoom-

ing in our development. You can already see the results."

"Part of that development, as you know, was the project on Mulliphen, to experiment with the Fault. I had no power over that project, and always openly opposed it for the reasons I just mentioned."

"Less than a year ago it came to my attention through Friend Chivon Lasster, who monitored results from the activities on Mulliphen, that a brilliant young quantaphys scientist was making inroads into the discovery of a new dimension in space. I have also been involved with the Walthor operation. As it happened, one of the scientists—Torlos Ornix—working with Calspar Shemzak—the previously mentioned quantaphys—had been fitted with a prosthetic bearing a spy device, and thus I could monitor his actions.

"In the course of contact with the Jaxdron, I mentioned this activity and they became deadly serious. Apparently they, too, wanted to pierce Omega Space, and they thought they could use Cal Shemzak. So I made a deal with them. We would allow them to invade Mulliphen without opposition and 'steal' Shemzak . . . as long as they destroyed the project and we were not allowed access to Omega Space. In return, I was to have more control over selecting Jaxdron targets, so that I could better monitor Federation military takeovers."

Zarpfrin shook his head and smiled ruefully. "Their response was absurd on the face of it, and yet I had to cooperate."

"What did they want?" asked Fernk, clearly astonished at all this.

"They said no, you make it too simple! We must make this a cat and mouse game. You must try and catch us, prevent our use of Cal Shemzak. I didn't know what to do, until I looked into Shemzak's records and discovered that his sibling was one of our XT pilots and an intelligence operative, with a fierce loyalty to the

fellow. I ran it through my stochastic computers an
came up with a quite byzantine plan that had a ver
good chance of snagging a particular headache of mine
Captain Tars Northern and the *Starbow*."

"Yes, yes," said Visto, gesturing to the document
hanging in the air. "We have many facts on the rest of i
. . . but apparently, all this has blown up in your face!"

"Perhaps," said Zarpfrin. "Not all has gone accord
ing to plan. But then, that is part of the fun of gaming,
suppose. But you must remember—I am in contact wit
the Jaxdron, and the *Starbow* is most certainly heade
to rescue Calspar Shemzak. Thus I have the final trump
card in my hand!"

"This is all preposterous, Zarpfrin!" said Mazerk
"You act as though you consider yourself our ruler
You have acted like a tyrant. Your machinations ar
deplorable and cannot be tolerated any longer. I vot
for an immediate censure, and must ask you to resig
from the Council and report for psychiatric readjust
ment after a full debriefing of your activities is made, s
that we can restore dignity and order!"

The response from the others was total agreement.

Zarpfrin shook his head sadly. "I'm sorry you fee
that way, gentles. In this you are confirming my deepes
suspicions that you're a thundering herd of doltheads
all of you!"

"Guards!" cried Visto. "Take this traitor away to hi
cell immediately. If he causes you trouble, you have ou
permission to sedate him."

But the guards did not respond as expected. Instead
they lowered their energy rifles and thumbed off th
safeties.

Zarpfrin stood and stepped back. "I am truly sorry
gentles, that it must be this way. But perhaps you ar
correct in one respect: I rather fancy the notion o
becoming a tyrant!"

"Now!" he said to the guards.

Overfriend Fernk went first, skewered on a rod of energy.

Almost simultaneously, Overfriend Mazerk's head was blasted off.

The other two rose.

Banili went for his intercom to call for help; the power beam that swept over him cut the man in two.

Overfriend Visto ran straight into a wall, as though he could run away through it. He turned around, his eyes wide with panic and terror. "You'll never get away with this, Zarpfrin!"

The power beams intersected where he stood, killing him in a blaze.

"People get so clichéd when they're about to die," Zarpfrin said. The air purification system struggled to suck away all the smoke and smell of burnt bodies.

Zarpfrin took out a handkerchief and blew his nose.

Chapter Nineteen

"You may call me Arnath," said one of the group of Frin'ral to Cal Shemzak and Ratham Bey, even as they goggled at the bizarre cityscape. The creature motioned with a meaty hand. "Come to our audience hall and we will speak on this matter before us."

"Anything you say," said Cal. "Come on, Ratham, I'm dying to find out more about this place."

Ratham nodded silently, following Cal.

They were led through a winding road flanked by the oddly tilted buildings, minarets, towers, and turrets. There was the delicious scent of cooking vegetables in the air; the smell of fresh flowers as they passed a pristine park centered by an ornate fountain, each stream of water shaded a different dazzling color. In the breeze the faint sound of distant wind chimes fluttered like gentle pleasant memories of lost melodies.

Occasionally they passed natives dressed in wildly different styles of clothing, but these natives in turn hardly took note of the visitors, as though it were an everyday event to see aliens upon the city streets.

"How does all this affect what you can do?" Ratham Bey asked.

"You mean, what we can do?" Cal replied.

"Yes, I mean the business of the mind." He waved around him. "You think this is all the product of their . . . wills?"

"For the most part I would think so. Let's see. I'm a little hungry. I'd like a hot dog."

He held out his hand, and in his palm there was a bun

with a cylinder of meat enclosed.

Complete with mustard.

"There, you see? However, I suppose that if I wanted to make that square building round, I wouldn't succeed. In other words, Ratham, what we have here is the result, no doubt, of consensus reality. The Frin'ral have created a town out of their imaginations."

"But each sees it in a slightly different way, which is why there is the skewed look to it."

"Exactly."

"So we had just better restrict ourselves to hot dogs and ice tea, to keep our noses clean."

"A wonderful idea."

"Why don't they just . . . beam us into this place?"

"Maybe this is the unguided tour of the town."

"Sort of showing off?"

"Who knows. Hard to say how these guys think."

They passed another park, where exotic birds roosted in feathery trees and unseen fauna made strange music in the underbrush.

Finally they were shown inside a large building carved from wood, with architectural aesthetics quite alien indeed. It seemed a collection of wooden petrified bubbles.

They were shown to a room and provided chairs. Two other Frin'ral sat in the room. One of them addressed the humans simply and directly: "Who are you and what are you doing here?"

Cal spoke up immediately: "Gee, you know, I could ask you the same thing."

"We are the Frin'ral. We have come here to . . . escape certain realities of the larger dimension. We were persecuted and pursued by a terrible race."

"I know how you feel," said Cal. "Well, this here is Lieutenant Ratham Bey. I'm Calspar Shemzak. We're human beings, and we certainly don't mean to pursue or persecute you. As for why we're here . . ."

Cal summed up the story as best he could, including the Jaxdron and the *Starbow* and how Ratham had fallen through the warp.

"And so you see, neither of us had any choice in the matter whatsoever."

"This is most disconcerting news—the Jaxdron attempting to pierce Omega Space . . . very upsetting."

"You know them, then?"

"Oh, yes we certainly do! They are the very race that drove us to seek refuge here," the apparent leader intoned.

"But why?"

"We would not play their games . . . or rather, we started playing their strange games, and then, when we realized what it was doing to our culture, we ceased. They are but spoiled children, the Jaxdron. They sought to wipe us out in vengeance for slighting them! And now they pursue us to the ends of time!"

"Don't worry," said Cal. "They needed me to get through, and I'm here, and I've closed the portal I used."

"This is good." The leader turned to Ratham Bey. "And we had vibrations to indicate that the portal you entered was destroyed, for it was booby trapped for the Jaxdron."

"I just hope that the others got out okay," said Ratham Bey, shivering. "But I should mention that one of your number, a fellow who calls himself Shontill, has been traveling with us, trying to get into Omega Space, trying to rejoin you!"

"Shontill!" They turned and looked at one another.

"You know him?"

"Our forefathers knew him. He was the stuff of history. But how is he yet alive?"

"Suspended animation. We found him in the wreckage of a spaceship, still ticking."

"He would be welcome back amongst us . . . yes, he

would," the leader intoned. "But the question remains now . . . what of the Jaxdron? You are sure you defeated them?"

"I didn't defeat them. I defeated their purpose."

"The Jaxdron seek vengeance upon us, yes, but they have other reasons to encroach upon Omega Space. They would wreak havoc here with their games. Ah, it would be terrible!"

"Yes," said Cal. "I understand what you mean. But the question remains, then . . . what can we do about them?"

"We have long been aware of this possibility," the Frin'ral said. "We are not unprepared. We are grateful for the warning. Now, we must ask you to cooperate."

"Cooperate in what?" asked Cal.

"We must work to first destroy this bunch of Jaxdron who used you. Then we must reseal the portal you opened."

Cal nodded. "Count me in."

Chapter Twenty

The day after the hairbreadth escape of the *Starbow* from the armada of Federation ships, Laura Shemzak lay in her cabin, reading.

She was still stunned at the turn of events. Despite her relief at no longer being addicted to Zernin, despite her near ecstasy at no longer having a malevolent voice inside her telling her what to do—a brief physical examination had shown the device to be destroyed; presumably by the Aspach during their spiritual occupation of her energy circuits—she still somehow felt weak and powerless, a pawn in some galactic game yet unfolding around her.

Whenever she had felt this way before during her service with the Federation, she would either visit with Cal or take a ride in a blip-ship. Now, though, Cal was far away; her blip-ship was wrecked, and besides, she couldn't fly it anyway.

She retreated to quietly lick her wounds. The book she stretched out with was a collection of poetry from ages long past. Tars Northern had let her borrow it from his collection.

"I'm sure you're used to spools and screens, but try reading something this way," he told her when she had inquired about reading matter. "It has its own peculiar pleasures . . . and the pictures are nice."

"Tars . . . I didn't know you liked poetry!"

"Yes. There's a good deal of human warmth and perception to the stuff that makes living in a tin can, slicing through nothingness, a little more bearable."

He'd been wearing his morning robe, looking older and very tired when she'd knocked at his cabin door, looking a little more vulnerable than usual.

"Thank you," she'd said. "Tars," she ventured. "Once all of this is through, if we're both alive . . . could we talk about us?"

"Us?" His eyes seemed to sparkle mischievously, awake at last.

"I've been through a great deal, and perhaps have to go through a great deal more before the end of it all. And, well, having Cal back is just not going to be enough. My feelings for him are of a quite different sort than my feelings for you. I'm starting to feel a need. . . ." Her words became nervous and hurried. "I don't want to be alone anymore. I mean, can you try to feel something for me? You've tried with others."

He frowned when he saw how serious she was. He motioned her to him, and put his arms around her—warmly, but paternally.

"Maybe I am starting to feel more than just healthy lust for you, Laura. But I'm not sure—"

"I just want to be with you more, Tars, know you better. I want to help you. It would get me out of myself, really it would!"

"Yes. That's an easy enough promise. We can spend more time together." He smiled easily. "I presume this means that you intend to stay on."

"Of course."

"And what about your brother?"

"He won't want to go back to the Federation. He can join the crew, can't he?"

"Are you so sure he'll want to, Laura? We're a pretty strange bunch."

"Oh he'll love it!"

"Just what we need—another eccentric."

"There's something else I need to talk to you about, Tars."

"By all means."

"When I was with Zarpfrin, down on Earth, he tried to break me with a bit of information."

"Sounds like the bastard. What was it, Laura?"

"That Cal is not really my brother. Cal just conned me because he thought having a sister was a terrific idea. He fixed the computer records. . . ."

Northern was quiet for a moment, considering. "Interesting fellow!"

"Well, it didn't bother me the way Zarpfrin wanted it to bother me. But now as I think about it . . ."

"It hurts?"

"In a way. He lied to me! He tried to control me, just like everyone else."

"Maybe he needed someone."

"Well, after he gets back safe and sound on board this ship and I give him a big hug and a wet kiss, I'm gonna slam him good!"

Northern laughed as he went to get a cup of morning coffee. "I just bet you will. Sounds to me as if you're going to survive that particular trauma. I'll tell you what, I'll get out a heavy blaster when he's here, and we'll hitch you two proper—a shotgun adoption!"

"You mean you'd make it official?"

"I'm the captain. I can do anything!"

"I'm not sure I want the little rat to be my brother anymore."

"You pout so very prettily, Laura." He offered her a cup of coffee. She refused.

"I'm off stimulants, remember?"

"Oh, yes." He sipped, and considered. "Is that why you're talking about getting closer to me? You want a new brother?"

"What?"

"A father?"

"Tars . . . I want *you!*"

"Relationships tend to be complex, and with complex emotional underpinnings."

"Hell with underpinnings!" she said, eyes flashing, anger boiling up. "I don't want a CompComp—I want a man!"

Northern chuckled. "Now there's the Laura I love! Yes, I don't think it would be too difficult to spend more time with you, should we manage to maintain our current molecular structure after this fracas!"

"Thanks," she said sarcastically. "Now I have something to live for!"

"You're the one who asked."

"You better watch out, Northern," she said, hefting the book. "This looks better to throw than a spool!"

"Oh, how do I love thee," the captain countered. "Let me count the ways!"

And so now Laura lay on her bed, sipping tea and letting the verses lazily wind through her mind like refreshing breezes.

There was a knock on the door that interrupted Keats's "Ode to a Grecian Urn."

"Hullo? Come in."

The door whisked open. Dansen Jitt nervously peeked in.

"Yes, Dans. What's up?"

"Captain's having a crew meeting in about two hours. He told me to check on you and tell you that."

"Thanks. Just reading some poetry. Come in, come in!"

The small man wandered in and was directed to sit in a chair beside the bed.

"Want some tea? Might calm you down."

Jitt accepted the tea.

"Just the usual jitters?"

"I need to talk to someone. Everyone else seems so preoccupied. I hate to ask, and I know that dumping all this on you is crummy after all you've been through—"

"Fire away. Things can't get too much worse than they've been."

Dansen Jitt looked morose as he began to sip the tea.

Naturally, he burned his tongue.

"After the fracas on Baleful—you remember?" he said, pausing to blow on his tea.

"How can I forget?"

"When I got that psychic message that told us where to pursue the Jaxdron?"

"Right," Laura said, encouraging him.

"It was more than that, Laura. I had a vision. The Jaxdron gave me a vision of what would happen at Snar'shill. I—" He sipped at his tea more successfully this time. "I saw a huge battle. Thousands of ships locked in struggle. And I saw you, smiling. . . ."

"Not unusual."

"And I saw the captain, Captain Northern, dead."

Laura mulled over that. "Clearly it's a trap, but knowing that, we might be able to use it to our advantage."

"But what about my vision?"

"You really believe the Jaxdron—"

"It was quite impressive."

"Must have been."

"They said something about joining their fun and games. I'm sorry to unload more on you, Laura, but I just had to talk."

Laura nodded. "I think it's a load of manure, myself. Games, you say, Jitt? This whole thing has been games within games from the beginning."

"But death is no game."

"Not if you're dead. But if you're living . . . so tell me, Dans. What are you suggesting? That we not go after them? That we run off with our tails between our legs?"

"I don't have a tail!"

"Figure of speech."

"I just don't like the idea of getting killed, that's all. Is that unnatural? Am I so inhuman as to be preoccupied with that?"

"No. I'm sorry."

Jitt shook his head. "No one understands. There are just things . . . things I see . . . things I dream. And they unnerve me! They'd unnerve anyone. I suppose you think I'm a coward, dying a thousand deaths instead of a hero's one. But it's not like that. No one believes me."

"You've had more of these precognitions lately?" Jitt nodded soberly.

"Right. So tell me about them!"

"A dream. I had a dream." Jitt looked up at her, meeting her eyes. "A dream about your brother."

"Tell me."

"I dreamed that somehow he had found the Frin'ral. Found Shontill's people. In a land as strange as strange gets."

"Omega Space!"

"It could be. And Laura . . . Ratham Bey was there too!"

"Lieutenant Ratham Bey? The guy that got sucked into that vortex on the abandoned Frin'ral ship?"

"That's him."

"What were they doing?"

"I'm not sure . . . just a glimpse, an impression of a bizzare city . . . but they seemed to be together peacefully."

"Amazing. Dans, how often are these psychic visions of yours true?"

"That's the problem, Laura. There's something in them that's always true. But I just can't get my interpretation right all the time."

Laura nodded. "That's why the captain razzes you so much. He's a perfectionist."

Jitt sighed. "Well, you really can't blame him. Like once, I envisioned this huge monster being inside a spaceship we were pirating. The boarding party was extra specially careful about that sector of this ship. The thing turned out to be Bickle, who Silver Zenyo took as a pet. The captain will never agree that my vision was correct, but that thing *is* an awful monster!''

Laura laughed. "Yes, I see. And your vision here doesn't make a whole lot of sense. But it does let us know that Cal's alive and possibly in contact with the Frin'ral.''

"Northern will just disregard it.''

"Well, I won't. I take it as a very encouraging vision indeed, Dansen. We will have to mention it at the meeting.''

"I really would rather you didn't. I don't know what good it would do the others. I just figured it might be reassuring to you.''

"That's very thoughtful of you, my friend. And about that other, horrific vision of yours—just think maybe you've got that one wrong as well.''

"I hope I don't have the part about you smiling wrong.''

Laura nodded. "The problem is, I've always said that I'm going to die with a smile on my face.''

Everyone looked a little weary and apprehensive at the open crew meeting. Even Captain Tars Northern seemed preoccupied—looking a bit more ruffled than usual, and notably without his usual drink.

As the general din of conversation quieted down in preparation for the meeting, Laura wondered whether the reason for Tars's preoccupation was Dr. Michael Mish.

Or rather, the change in Dr. Mish.

From the time the robot extension of the *Starbow* entered the room, the change in personality was discernible. Rather than the frowsy, absentminded doctor Laura had first met, he was neatly dressed and totally self-possessed. There seemed about him an aura of completeness, power, and awareness of things beyond normal ken. When his eyes lit upon anything, there was a look of analysis in that look.

This troubled Laura. She had liked Dr. Mish's personality. He still had certain fatherly qualities about him, but they were not as pleasing as before. Stern, Old Testament stuff here, as Cal might have said.

The first person who took an immediate interest in Mish's new presence was Chivon Lasster, who stepped up and engaged in immediate quiet conversation with him, an intense expression on her face. She seemed to want to hug him, but obviously restraining herself, she did not. Mish ended the dialogue by squeezing her arm, then taking his place beside the captain.

Laura immediately noticed that there was no monitor in Mish's hands. He hardly seemed interested in Northern's condition. The pair clearly did not have the rapport they had once shared, and Northern seemed a bit lost because of it.

Plainly, joining with his fellow Aspach had made Mish into a different kind of creature. Laura wondered if this was good or bad as Captain Tars Northern called the meeting to order.

"This is just a general information meeting, and an opportunity for all involved to present observations and suggestions," he began.

"As you might have gathered, we are now finally headed toward Snar'shill. I'm sure you are all aware this has been our destination for some time. We have taken a few detours since we first learned of that destination, but all those detours have been eminently to our advantage."

"Not much good for our nerves, though!" called out a young ensign.

Northern smiled ruefully. "Did anyone ever promise anyone here that joining up with the *Starbow* crew was going to prove to be a nerve tonic?"

"Plenty of rum, though!" cried the ensign.

"Yes. Well, we're pirates, aren't we, mateys? Now, then . . . we are all going to have to take part in this upcoming assault on what will presumably be a Jaxdron base. As we no longer have our blip-ship in service, we are going to have to rely on our pinnaces, rigged with as much firepower as possible, to be our fighters once again. And we shall have to use the *Starbow* itself."

"The *Starbow*? How is that going to help?" asked Gemma Naquist. "I mean sure, yeah, if we deal with the odd Jaxdron ship in Snar'shill's system, it will be quite effective, but for assaulting an alien base?"

"It will all become plain in a moment," said Northern. "First, let me introduce to you Dr. Michael Mish, or should I say, the new Dr. Michael Mish. Our rescue operation for his fellow Aspach was completely successful. All are now joined together within the *Starbow* . . . hopefully quite compatibly, Mish?"

Dr. Mish nodded. He seemed about to smile in the old Mish fashion, but suppressed it.

"Well, excellent. So essentially what we have here is no longer an intelligent, self-aware starship trying to come to grips with its identity and its powers, but a new being, in full possession of its faculties . . . and no doubt with a great deal to tell us . . . including the answers to the question in regarding the *Starbow*'s role in confronting the Jaxdron base. Dr. Mish, if you would do us the honor."

The crew applauded lightly as Dr. Mish stood up.

"You must understand," he said, "this is still all rather confusing at this time—five becoming one, with the four of us unaccustomed to being a space vessel again. For years we were fugitives in the computer systems of Earth, afraid to be found out—and now we are amongst friends again. This is good, and it is good to be a ship again, and good to have within us good people like you. Together, we shall form a truly unique composite creature, working for good in the dimensions!"

"Oh," said Laura. "Good!"

Northern shot her a withering glare.

"Yes," continued Mish. "Good, indeed. Alas, there are still mysteries to be uncovered as to our origins and the meaning of the portal that is our core, and who exactly created us . . . but all that will come. It will come when it is time.

"But now, to the matter at hand.

"As you know, we have been seeking this place called Omega Space just as much as the Jaxdron. To find Cal Shemzak, to discover attilium, to thwart the Jaxdron—these are our goals.

"As you have discovered, there are qualities to the *Starbow* that you have discovered bit by bit, including its ability to use Underspace to jump directly into and directly out of a significant gravity well. This is a power that the Federation—and apparently the Jaxdron—do not possess, and thus we may use it to great advantage in dealing with both groups.

"However, the matter immediately before us concerns the methods by which we will directly engage the Jaxdron in their base, where they are keeping Cal Shemzak."

"Yes," said Silver Zenyo. "Like how we're going to accomplish that little feat without getting ourselves blown down into Omega Space!"

The old Dr. Mish might have chuckled at that one; the new merely stared at the woman. "Alas, that is a very real possibility."

"Oh, gee, thanks," said Dansen Jitt as he fiddled with his pen agitatedly. "That helps a lot!"

"Uhm, Doctor, I really think you've got much to learn in your new . . . persona, shall we say," the captain said, then stood and waved the murmuring crew to silence. "This isn't the first time we've run into a tight situation! What's the problem?"

"You're right," said Silver. "It's just that we're used

to a little more self-confidence from the brass!''

Dr. Mish looked bemused. ''I merely relate facts.''

''Carry on, Doctor,'' said Northern. ''We'll just have to go with the punches.''

''Very well. As previously mentioned, we are discovering more and more concerning our . . . our body, shall we call it. The *Starbow*. This ship. When we were first awakened from our sleep of countless millennia, all of us were confused. It was very easy for us to acquiesce to the Federation's request that our bodies be rebuilt, that we should find ways in which to express our individualities, and that we should disguise our personalities as the result of Artificial Intelligence Experiments. Perhaps if we owned our full faculties at the time, we would have seen what was coming. . . .

''However, we are more prepared to deal with situations such as the one before us now, due to our combined state and also to our stay within Earth computers where—although we dared to do only what was necessary—we learned a great deal about the Federation.''

''Okay, okay!'' someone shouted. ''So how about the Jaxdron base?'

''Oh, yes,'' said Mish. ''Our personalities are not totally combined as of yet, and we tend to go off on tangents. It's very simple. We have discovered that the *Starbow* can land on planets.''

The entire crew stared at him, aghast.

Except for Northern, who was smiling.

''What?'' said Arkm Thur. ''That's impossible. I've made a detailed study of this ship. Structurally it is simply not—''

Captain Northern raised his hand. ''Let the doctor continue, if you please. . . .''

''To finish Mr. Thur's statement, it is, of course, impossible for the *Starbow* to enter the atmosphere of a planet normally. However, such is the power and control of our Underspace engines and our force-fields that we can literally transfer to a point above the surface and then land if we choose to do so.''

"But that's still impossible. The hull . . . those damn spokes!''

"You were not able to do a full study of this ship, Mr. Thur. The spokes on the 'bottom' of the ship are retractable, allowing for landing on a flat surface. As for the hull . . .'' He paused. "You must stop thinking about this spaceship as though it were human-built. You must approach it more as an organic entity . . . and thus we can change many details of our design, including the makeup of our hull.''

"Incredible,'' said Thur, shaking his head with wonder.

"Wait a minute,'' said Laura. "Are you trying to tell me that we're gonna rescue Cal by sheer force?''

"Remarkably astute, young lady. That's entirely correct,'' responded Dr. Mish.

"That's right, my friends,'' Northern affirmed. "We're going to land this delightful ship, let the Jaxdron base have it—presuming there is a Jaxdron base, of course—and simply storm it!''

"That's the sum total of our strategy?'' Gemma Naquist said, aghast.

"Well, naturally our strategy depends on what our sensors show us,'' Northern said. "But we've looked at the situation as carefully as we can. We have discovered that not only can the *Starbow* do impossible things, it also has a hell of a lot more firepower than we thought. It's a shame we can't spend some more time just discovering the full extent of our power, but we've used up enough time already and must strike just as soon as possible.''

"Yes,'' Mish concurred. "Analysis of previous forays with the Jaxdron show that we have attained sufficient battle status in order to directly confront them.''

"Let me get this straight,'' Laura said. "We land. We

blow a hole in their base. We storm it and rescue Cal. But what about this Omega Space business? Haven't you gotten anything more on that?''

''Alas, as I said, although we are progressing significantly,'' said Mish, ''we need Cal Shemzak.''

''Hey, wait a minute,'' said Laura. ''We've been mucking about so much, we haven't thought of this one—what if Cal and the Jaxdron have *already* gotten into Omega Space?''

''There is the possibility of the former,'' said Dr. Mish. ''However, as to the latter . . . no.''

''I don't understand,'' said Gemma Naquist.

''Perhaps, Doctor, we should bring out our guest speaker.'' Captain Northern turned and consulted with one of the robots, General MacArthur. The robot scurried from the room.

''Guest speaker?'' said Silver Zenyo, looking around quizzically. ''As far as I can tell, the whole crew is here!''

''Not entirely,'' said Northern.

General MacArthur returned to the room. Behind him was a man.

Or rather, at first sight, it was a man. A very tall man.

At first sight Laura Shemzak did not recognize the person, but then two added itself to two, and the inevitable conclusion arrived.

The ''man'' did not sit down, but stood behind Mish and Northern, as though contritely awaiting his turn to speak.

It was Shontill!

Chapter Twenty-one

Fingersnap fast, the Frin'ral city was no more.

Cal Shemzak found himself and the rest of the party —five Frin'ral and Ratham Bey—sitting in the plain field.

They sat in a circle around the two-dimensional black circle that marked the aperture between Omega Space and Alpha Space.

The Frin'ral began to chant.

"What the hell is going on?" asked Bey.

"Some sort of ceremony, looks like," said Cal.

"What's that thing in the air?"

Cal explained.

"Ah . . . so we're getting ready to open it again."

"I don't know. I'm not sure how they're going to handle the Jaxdron when it opens."

"Can you do that by yourself?"

Cal thought about that, reaching into his awareness, setting up the matrix again.

"Yes," he said finally.

The chant continued, quite unmusical to Cal's ears, almost dirgelike.

"Funny," said Bey. "I'm not frightened. I should be frightened, but I'm not frightened."

"Yes," said Cal. "I noticed that too."

"A little excited . . . expectant. Like something very fascinating and fulfilling is going to happen. Giddy maybe . . . full of anticipation."

"Anticipation," mused Cal. "Yes."

The spokesman of the Frin'ral opened his eyes. "Please prepare to join our collective trance. There are things that you both must understand before we ask you to reopen the portal, Calspar Shemzak—aspects of ourselves as yet unknown to you."

"Trance?" said Rathan Bey. "Now, I'm scared."

"What?"

"Just kidding." But Bey did look alarmed.

"What must we do?" asked Cal.

"Nothing. Just do not be alarmed at the seeming physical aspects and the sensations of falling into otherness. You will be quite safe."

"I guess we've seen worse, haven't we, Cal?"

Cal nodded, and almost immediately began slipping away into the chant, sliding into a montage of images and voices and sensory impressions that told the tale of the Frin'ral.

It seemed he was in the trance for a very long time . . . or rather, the time he spent was timeless. When he finally reemerged, he felt as though he had awoken from a faint.

As reality began to collect around him, he turned to Ratham Bey and said, "Wow!"

Bey was speechless.

The Frin'ral in the circle were all watching him.

"Let me get this straight. This wasn't just a hallucination, was it?"

"In a way, perhaps," answered one. "But the hallucination represented the truth."

Cal shook his head as though to clear it.

"The Frin'ral and the Terrans—we're related? I mean, we're sort of galactic distant cousins? I'm not sure I get it. I saw images I just couldn't understand."

"We are both races planted by the Seeders. Even we know little of the Seeders, though it was they who created the races of intelligent life in the galaxies. They are long gone now. Long gone. A mystery."

"But the Frin'ral and humanity—we're both of the same genetic stock?"

'That is correct, only the Frin'ral adapted through evolution into their present form in a different environment. There is a state in the maturation of an adult, in fact, when a Frin'ral looks quite human. This is during the breeding years of the male's life."

"Shontill! Kinda human . . . incredible!"

"Yeah," said Cal. "It makes us all brothers under the scales, doesn't it?"

"But the story . . . the history . . . I didn't quite grasp it."

"We shall summarize," the Frin'ral spokesman said. "The Frin'ral developed much as humanity developed. There are analogous phases of our history, in fact. But when we started exploring the stars, creating colonies, growing, we were much more advanced in certain areas. By that time we were quite aware of the existence of Omega Space, and we were a great deal less warlike than you humans.

"But at that point, we met the Jaxdron.

"The Jaxdron wished to play war games . . . space war games."

"Yeah, tell us about the Jaxdron," said Cal eagerly. "I don't know a hell of a lot about them, even though I was their prisoner."

"The Jaxdron are the immature state of a larger race called the Maxtron."

"Huh?" said Cal.

"Immature state?" said Bey.

"They are what you might classify as teenagers," said the Frin'ral spokesman.

"And their parents have given them the car!" Cal said. "Of course! Incredible! But it makes a kind of kooky sense."

"Yes. They have no desire for territory per se, they just wish to play . . . and to make the stakes as real as possible. We made the mistake of refusing to play with them. They had a temper tantrum and began destroying our planets.''

"For years we had been working on the possibilities of entering Omega Space. Our problems with the Jaxdron forced us to work harder on the problem, and we succeeded. By that time we had grown few in number, and the Jaxdron outclassed us in weaponry in every way . . . so we escaped here.''

"All except for Shontill," said Bey. "But wait a moment. How come Shontill didn't know all this?"

"Only the very top rulers of our people knew the whole truth. To the others, including Shontill, it was a simple space war which we were losing. They had no idea of the absurdity of the whole business!''

"Absurd is right," mused Cal. "Just to think—teenagers!''

"It is, of course, more complex than that, but these are the words that you may understand the best.''

"So the brats still want to wipe you out?"

"Now, we believe, they just wish to control Omega Space, and we are in the way.''

"So, how are we going to do this? You want me to open the portal now?" Cal asked.

"No. Now is not the correct time. We must wait until the right moment.''

"Right moment? What's wrong with now? I want to get those bastards.''

"That will not be necessary.''

"Huh? What are you talking about?"

"Our probing of normal space indicates that the arrival of another party on Snar'shill is imminent. We will wait until then.''

"Arrival?" said Ratham Bey.

"Laura!" said Cal. "Laura and the *Starbow*. It's got to be them.''

He grinned, and rubbed his hands together expectantly.

Chapter Twenty-two

When they emerged from Underspace, they found themselves hanging in orbit of a Class M planet remarkably like Earth.

A quick sensory sweep of the area by the *Starbow* revealed no evidence of Jaxdron ships. The planet was apparently unguarded. That it was Snar'shill, there was no doubt; but the lack of any kind of precautions by the enemy made Captain Northern suspicious.

It took only a couple of hours to locate the Jaxdron surface base. The *Starbow* analyzed it as best it could, and its occupants made their strategic and tactical decisions. Calculations were accomplished. Coordinates were set.

"Well," said Captain Northern. "All stations alert?"

Everyone was at battle stations. Pinnace crews reported all ready. The gunners were in place.

Northern turned to Dr. Mish. "Time to see if this little power of yours really works. The ship is prepared?"

"Adaptations for atmospheric entry have been made," answered Mish.

"Right." He secured himself in his Captain's chair. "Geronimo!"

"Or at the very least, Crazy Horse!" said Dansen Jitt nervously.

"Hm." A glimmer of the old Mish returned to the robot's eyes. "Two generals I have neglected . . . Plenty of time, though. Plenty of time."

Despite this digression, the officers at the controls understood and instantly keyed the preprogrammed orders.

The view of the planet Snar'shill dissolved in the observation screens . . .

. . . to be replaced by a close-up of the landscape and a large metallic-and-cement building only five hundred meters distant.

The Jaxdron base, thought Laura Shemzak as she watched from her station in the pinnace, crammed into her battle armor. In her excitement she had forgotten the discomfort.

The *Starbow* hung for a time fifty meters above the grassy surface, the bottom spokes retracting, gun sights aimed at the nearest wall of the Jaxdron compound.

At Northern's order, the onslaught of energy was unleashed, crackling mercilessly against the walls. Chunks of material blew into the sky. Smoke gushed up. When the smoke cleared, a gaping hole stood in the wall.

"No force screens?" Captain Northern said.

"I admit bafflement as well," said Dr. Mish. "There is no defense activity whatsoever evident. The Jaxdron ships in that field yonder are unmanned. Yet sensors detect definite inhabitation of life within the walls."

"An aspect of a trap?"

"A trap was what we expected, Captain. If it is a trap prepared for us, it appears to be a very bad one!"

"Then you would recommend continuation of the attack?"

"Absolutely, Captain."

"Right. Deploy raiding parties!" he ordered.

The orders went down to the three pinnaces, and the docking bay doors swung open.

"Okay, you guys," Laura Shemzak said to the five robots under her command. "Let's get this boat going!"

She was strapped into a seat behind the pilot, feeling damned uncomfortable not being in control of the rig. Not enough time for training, and besides, as leader of this squadron, she had to concentrate on the task of taking it through that hole, dealing with any Jaxdron defense . . . and then finding Cal. No time to worry about running a rocket-ship. Still, she missed the sense of complete control she had in her XT, that feeling of power. Even in sturdy battle armor, she felt extremely vulnerable.

Hannibal, the pilot, went through the ignition procedures, while Eisenhower, the gunner, sat by him making sure his guns were ready. They fairly shone with military competence, yet Laura was still impatient. "C'mon guys, let's hustle it up so we can hit 'em while their pants are down!" she commanded.

"Operating at optimum efficiency," Hannibal said even as his fingers manipulated the banks of controls. "I suggest the human quality of patience."

"Patience! My brother is in there!" She examined the other robots. "Your guns ready to blast?"

"Yes," they answered in unison.

"Good. I wanna see some Jaxdrons getting their first taste of hellfire!"

Soon, the pinnace thundered up on its antigravs and retros, navigated through the doors and took its position beside the other pinnaces hovering a hundred yards beyond the *Starbow*.

"Any signs of activity?" Laura radioed Gemma Naquist in the next ship.

"None," was the response.

"Okay if I go first?"

"Are you sure you're ready for that kind of thing?" Arkm Thur asked from the other boat.

"I'm about as ready as I'll ever be. Besides, I'm better at this than you guys."

"Also more humble," returned Thur.

Laura led the raiding team through the blasted hole into a larger chamber. At first there was no defense. But when all three pinnaces had landed, a door opened and fighting machine robots erupted, holding blasters.

The Jaxdron robots were only able to get off a few

blasts before the pinnace lasers blew them apart. They continued streaming out and as they did, the pinnaces picked them off easily until all that was left was a smoking pile of rubble.

"No further robot activity detected on sensors," Eisenhower declared.

"Okay," said Laura. "Let's land and get this over with."

The pinnaces put down. Within moments all but the pilots had run down the ramps, collecting into a single party. "How's it going, Lasster?" asked Laura. Chivon Lasster had insisted on accompanying the raiding party. She had gone with Arkm Thur.

"You don't forget how to do this kind of thing," the woman answered. "You just forget how exciting it can be!"

Laura grunted with approval. This lady might turn out to be okay. She might even survive, if she kept her hands off the captain.

Still, Arkm Thur was looking at her in a peculiar way. Fondly? Laura sure as hell hoped so!

"Still want to go first?" Gemma Naquist asked, adjusting her helmet.

"You bet," said Laura. "C'mon!"

They picked their way over the remains of the Jaxdron robots, into the next room.

They met no more.

"I don't understand," said Arkm Thur. "Why so little opposition?"

"Mish said something about the Jaxdron being preoccupied," answered Laura. "Let's see."

Laura at the lead, the party blasted through the next door, and found itself in a long corridor.

"What you got on your sensors?" asked Laura.

Eisenhower looked down, fiddling with the flat device. "Definite biological life activity at the end of this hall."

They made their way three by three, weapons ready.

At the end of the hall, another door opened. More robots, more guns.

"Good heavens," said Chivon Lasster, raising her gun.

"Take cover!" Laura ordered.

"What cover?" Naquist asked, but she knew what Laura meant.

The humans in the party stepped behind the less vulnerable robots. Laura pulled her weapon up, found the closest robot in the cross hairs and pulled the trigger. Energy erupted like the blossoming of a deadly flower. The fire slammed into the metallic torso of the thing, but did little more than warm it up a bit. Laura kept the blast up.

With a little smile; Lasster winked at Laura through the vuport of her armor, lifted her gun and let the robot have it right between its optical sensors. The blast caused the robot to stagger back. Lasster swung her beam down, blasting off one of the nodes extending from its neck. The robot, with a keening screech and a halo of radiation, stumbled, then crashed to the floor.

"Not in the chest, Laura. You must find their vulnerable parts."

"Yeah," said Laura, exasperated at not thinking of this sooner. She turned her attention to a robot racing close, calmly drew a bead on one of its neck nodes, and slammed some firepower where it counted. The blast tore off the node. The robot kept coming, screeching metallically. Calmly, Laura raised the crackling beam, cutting a burning scar up the thing's "face" until the full power was crashing into the thing's optical sensors. That stopped it!

The robot began a strange little dance, and then, with the welcome help of a few additional beams, went down for the count.

Suddenly a beam of fire erupted from out of nowhere, slashing straight into Hannibal's face-plate, slamming him back so hard against a wall that he fell to pieces.

Chivon Lasster fell to the floor, rolled to avoid the zig-zagging beam, then nailed the bastard who was delivering it. *Hot damn*, thought Laura. *There's a lot more to this woman than I thought!*

Slashes and gashes of fire crisscrossed madly for what seemed like only moments, but must have been minutes. Smoke was billowing. Crashes and screechings echoed through the hallway. The servo-motors in Laura's battle suit strained to deal with the smoke and the exertion she was placing on them.

Then suddenly, with a hiss and a wail, the din stopped.

Slowly, the smoke dissipated.

The Jaxdron robots were now just rubble strewn over the floor. Here and there a joint squeaked, and digits twitched, but sensors showed the things to be no further threat.

The *Starbow* party had lost only two of its robots in the melee, and none of the humans had even been scratched. They were a little uncomfortable and worn-out in their overheated suits. A small price to pay for victory, though!

"Good job," said Laura.

"Life signs continue," reported Eisenhower.

"Anything resembling human life signs?" asked Laura.

"Not detectable."

"Let's go check this out anyway!" Laura declared, adjusting her power gun for another round of fighting. She turned and looked at Chivon Lasster. "Thanks. You're pretty damned good at this."

"You forget, I've had Federation commando training," responded Chivon coolly. "And I've kept in practice. You'd be surprised at the military and action-training needed to push papers!'' She smiled, warming.

"Well, I'm just glad we're on the same side now, dearie,'' said Laura, checking her weapon's power supply.

"I'm finding it's a good side to be on."

They made their way to the end of the corridor, and through the door.

There was no sign of any more robots. But a terrible din was coming from the end of the other corridor they had entered: the sound of fighting.

"What the hell is going on?" Arkm Thur wondered out loud.

Laura could not hide her alarm. "Must be something to do with Cal. Let's hit it!"

She ran ahead of the party, the heavy pounding of her battle suit echoing in the empty corridor.

After two turns of the hallway, she was confronted by the sight of a Jaxdron robot hurtling from a room. It crashed against a wall so hard that it burst into pieces.

Smoke issued from the room . . . smoke and roars.

She sprinted for the door. There she saw something even more incredible.

A gigantic cartoonish bunny rabbit was battling a group of Jaxdron robots.

At least twelve feet tall, it had droopy ears and goofy eyes and long fearsome teeth. It was colored purple and red.

She'd seen this kind of thing before. Cal had used to draw them with magic markers when he was younger.

The beams the robots shot at this demented-looking beast seemed to deflect magically from its furry hide. One by one it caught them up in his giant paws and smashed them against the wall, or stomped them with its huge feet until they were just piles of rubble.

Then Laura noticed the portal behind her, like a large sparkle-edged mirror, reflecting something entirely different from what was in the room.

By the time the others had joined her, she was over her surprise.

"What the devil . . . ?" murmured Gemma.

"No, it's just a giant bunny rabbit," said Laura. "Let's help it."

She and Chivon began blasting away at the Jaxdron robots. The other robots did likewise, but Gemma Naquist and Arkm Thur were so baffled by the sight before them that by the time they were able to raise their own weapons, all the enemy robots in the room had been dispatched.

The giant bunny rabbit began giggling as it settled back on its haunches. "Better be ready," it said. "They'll probably have more heading our way."

"Cal," said Laura, walking forward. "What have they done to you?"

"Oh, this really isn't me, Laura. It's just a projection from Omega Space. Here, let me put it out of the way so that I can scramble through and say hello properly."

The giant rabbit grinned sheepishly.

And then suddenly it just wasn't there anymore.

Instead, all that was left was the portal, about two meters high, hanging in the air.

A hand reached over its sparkling lip.

Another hand, a head.

Cal Shemzak pulled himself up and over, flopping onto the ground.

"Cal," cried Laura, trudging forward ecstatically.

"Mmmmmph," said Cal, struggling to get up.

Laura grabbed him and squeezed him in a bear hug, forgetting the power of the servo-motors in the armor she wore.

"Urrghh," said Cal. "Stop!"

"Oh, sorry." She let him go and then stepped back. "You *are* Cal, aren't you? Calspar Shemzak?"

Cal leaned over, his breathing raspy. "Of course I'm Cal, you ninny! Who else could I be?"

"Like maybe one of those Jaxdron-tailored Cal clones."

"How'd you know about those?"

"It's a long story. But Cal . . . It really is you? We've come such a long way . . . It's so hard to believe!"

"You think that's hard to believe?" He gestured toward what lay beyond the portal. "*That's* what's hard to believe."

"That's Omega Space?" said Gemma Naquist, drifting forward. "That's what we've been searching for all this time?"

"It looks like Kansas!" said Arkm Thur.

"No. Definitely more like Oz." He turned around and looked in. "Hey, Ratham. Your friends are here. Come on through."

And Ratham Bey struggled through, looking much the same as he had when he had fallen into the center of the Frin'ral ship.

"Hi, guys," he said. "Thanks for showing up." He peered around. "What about the robots?"

"I think we destroyed most of them," said Arkm Thur.

"A wonderful thought. But the Jaxdron . . . what about them?"

"I've met the suckers. They're much too weak on their own to be any threat," said Cal.

"We should find them before they do something else," said Laura. "Like maybe escape."

She quickly alerted the *Starbow*, reporting on what had happened, and then informing them about the possibility of a Jaxdron escape.

"Oh, that's okay," Captain Northern's voice crackled. "I've just taken the liberty of finding the vessels. They won't fly more than two meters now."

Cal clapped his hands together. "Wonderful! Can anyone let me borrow their gun? I've got a few repayments to make here."

"No, Cal. We've got to capture them. Alive, they'll tell us a lot."

Cal's eyes got big and wicked-looking. "Yeah!"

"Can you keep this portal open for a while, Cal?"

"Oh, sure . . . As long as my brain is plugged into the clone array." His face grew concerned. "We'd better hurry. They might try to destroy it."

"We'll station a couple of robots here," Laura said. "You'd better come and show us where the Jaxdron are, Cal."

"No problem. Bey, you stay here. Any problem, just sic Bugs on 'em like I showed you."

"How did you do that?" Laura asked.

"I'll tell you later. It has a lot to do with Omega Space."

"Right," said Laura. "I'd give you a kiss, but this helmet is hell to get out of."

"It'll keep. Let's go!"

Bey grinned. "Can I make my own monster next time?"

Chapter Twenty-three

Laura and her comrades crept through the halls, looking for any sign of the Jaxdron or their robots. It was quiet—perhaps too quiet.

Cal listened to Laura's story of how the *Starbow* had surprised the Jaxdron. "They must have been so wrapped up in trying to figure out how to use my clone matrix to get their tails into Omega Space, they didn't guard them properly," he said. "Anyway, my evaluation of them is that they're really not the fierce beasties the Federation has been touting them as. They're not exactly on my list of favorite things in the universe, though . . . ."

"Yeah," said Laura.

They threaded their way though silent corridors, following the directions that Cal had given them. Several minutes passed. Laura breathed a sigh of relief. Maybe the Jaxdron weren't the heavy hitters everyone thought they were! She relaxed as they negotiated the last bit, turning amused thoughts to a roomful of Calspar Shemzaks.

But the Jaxdron had not left themselves unguarded. There were twelve of them. Robots. Significantly superior to the others, capable no doubt of all kinds of mayhem. The search party stopped short, bringing up their weapons.

The robots advanced, aiming power weapons at the party. Laura caught her breath, cursing her stupidity. But the metal army did not fire. Laura was more than surprised when one well-armed robot stepped forward and spoke.

"Greetings, Humans of the *Starbow*. How very well played! A most remarkable Game. We despise losing, but of course, in recapturing the principal playing piece, Cal Shemzak, you have accomplished a remarkable endgame, and we are forced to resign. So now, if you take Mr. Shemzak wherever you like, we can repair our ships and be on our way, never to bother you again."

"That's what you think, buster!" Laura let the spokesrobot have it with a scorching pulse of power. Energy rays sizzled through the air.

"Cal!" called Laura to her unarmored brother. "Get back. Around the corner!"

Cal pivoted wide-eyed to run, but slipped. A robot arm swiveled automatically, tracking the action. It was glowing, getting ready to fire. Laura was too far away to be of any help.

"Cal!" she screamed, tracking her own beam toward the enemy robot.

In a flash, though, another armor suit was hurtling toward Cal. The robot weapon unleashed its energies—and the battle suit caught them full in the back of its neck.

It was Chivon Lasster's suit!

The blast knocked off a few attachments and sent Chivon spinning head over heels to crash into a wall. Cursing, Laura swung her beamer the rest of the way, blowing off the Jaxdron robot's head.

"Chivon!" cried Arkm Thur, dodging a beam and letting one of his own slam into the enemy. He bounded back to where the former Friend lay in a heap against a wall.

"Ouch!" said Chivon Lasster. Even from where she stood, Laura could see the blood running from her mouth. "I thought these things were supposed to absorb the blows . . ."

"Are you all right, Lasster?" Laura shouted above the sizzling din of weapons fire.

"Just banged up!"

Thur was bending over her. "She's more than that," he said, reading a dial. "But her life functions are strong."

"Can she walk?" Laura blasted a robot, moving behind one of her own.

"Sure," said Chivon, her voice weaker.

"Well, get her back to a pinnace and ferry her back to the *Starbow*. And, Chivon . . ."

"Yes?"

"You die and I'm going to kick your butt."

"Thanks, Laura. I don't think I could take that indignity."

Laura covered them as they staggered off back to the pinnace.

"Hey, they could have left me one of those suits!" said Cal. "I feel naked."

"Shut up and stay out of range," said Laura, readjusting her blaster. "We've got a little blasting to do!"

Energy rays sliced through the air. Laura was more than thankful for her battle armor as she again entered the fray. Rays caromed off walls, splattering molten metal. Laura shouted encouragment to Gemma Naquist and their robots. "Let's crush these tin cans!" she cried, aiming at a Jaxdron robot. The energy beam coursed from her gun, blowing the robot to pieces. She turned quickly, fired from the hip and reduced another to metal scrap. Gemma took out another.

As the smoke cleared over the burning wreckage and insulation, Laura could see that all the Jaxdron robots had been wrecked. Mish's robots must have been of superior design, because only three more, including Eisenhower, alas, had been casualties, their parts and burning bits mingled with the enemy's.

"How's Lasster doing?" Laura radioed to Thur.

"We're in the pinnace," Thur answered. "I've got most of her suit off, and we're applying first aid. She's

still conscious. Burns, a concussion maybe. I think a
broken rib. Nothing Mish won't be able to heal."

"Good. I owe her. And so does Cal, the miserable
klutz."

Cal stepped from behind a corner, waving away the
smoke. "Sorry."

"I should have sent you back with them."

"You can't, remember? I have to lead you to the
Jaxdron chamber."

"Well then, that's what you'll have to do."

Cal picked up Chivon's fallen rifle. "Just in case!"

Laura waited for the metal and floor to cool down
before she ordered the survivors to advance into the
next chamber.

They found the Jaxdron in their float-fields. Laura
was surprised at how funny looking they were.

"You jerks are about as fearsome-looking as side-
show critters!" She stood in the middle of the room,
gun up and ready. "Consider yourself prisoners of
war!" she said.

The Jaxdron raised their probosci simultaneously.

"A gesture of surrender?" Laura asked the others.

"No, Laura Shemzak," said the middle Jaxdron. "A
gesture of bemusement. You play your games in very
strange ways. We have resigned, and yet you destroy
our servants, making us helpless."

"This is no game!!" said Laura. "And we're going to
put an end to the other games you've been playing as
well!"

"Are those the conditions of our defeat?"

The radio sputtered on. Gemma lifted her unit and
responded. Captain Northern's voice sounded.

"*Starbow* to raiding party, *Starbow* to raiding party.
Over."

"You've got us," said Naquist. "And we've got our
guns trained on a bunch of strange-looking creatures
who are apparently the Jaxdron. You want us to bring
them aboard?"

"Negative. Leave them there. Mish's orders. He's got an idea . . ."

"An idea?" Laura said, angry.

"Yes. Seems that because of all this, we may well actually be able to use the Jaxdron. They're probably pretty pissed at the Federation by now. They might want to war in earnest with ole Zarpfrin and the Best Buddies. And we don't have time to take any captives. Get Cal Shemzak and Ratham Bey, and bring them back immediately."

"After all this trouble, you just want us to let them *go*?" Laura said disbelievingly. "What's the problem?"

"Sensors have indicated a number of starships approaching Snar'shill. We are presuming them to be a Federation fleet."

"So soon?" Laura said.

"Yes. Presumably Earth alerted nearby vessels to head here after our successful escape."

"How long have we got?"

"Not long. Okay?

"But what about the Jaxdron?"

"Just leave them. Let the Federation deal with them. Oh . . . and you're going to have a visitor. I'm sending Shontill out. He can join his people now."

"Right, Captain. Over and out." She glared up at the aliens. "You jerks are in luck. We apparently are ending the game the way you want!"

"Excellent! We thought you would come around to the natural way of looking at things," replied the Jaxdron spokesman.

"So you'd better just sit there and be good or we will just go ahead and blow this place apart!"

"Understood."

"Come on, Gemma. You too, Cal."

Calspar Shemzak was staring at his weapon. "There's something wrong with this thing, Laura. And I don't want it to not work if we meet up with more robots." He fiddled with a lever. "I . . ."

Suddenly, an intense blast of energy slammed through the air from the nozzle. It smashed into the Jaxdron leader. The creature exploded, fiery bits and pieces flying all over the others. Their float-fields destroyed, the others crashed to the floor and scrambled to get away.

"Oops!" said Cal.

Laura stepped forward and snatched the rifle from Cal's grasp. She stared at him for a moment. "You're going to have to learn to follow orders from now on, Cal." She nodded sadly at him, understanding in her eyes. Then she turned to the others. "Right. My orders are not to report this incident." She spun on her heel and motioned for the others to follow her back to the room in which they had left Ratham Bey.

"You found them?" asked Ratham Bey when Laura and the others returned.

"You bet." She smiled smugly.

"What happened. What did you do?"

"Nothing. No time. We've gotta get out of here. Federation ships closing in."

"You didn't kill them?"

"No."

"Okay," said Cal. "I guess we'd better split."

At that moment, Shontill arrived in a very agitated state.

"My people . . . this portal . . . ah!" he said, seeing the opening before him.

"I take it this is Shontill?" Cal asked Ratham.

"He's changed a bit," Ratham said, unable to hide his astonishment.

"Yeah. Would have changed permanently if not for Dr. Mish," said Laura. "Well, Shontill. That's it. Jump on through if you like. Cal tells me that's where your people are. Good luck."

The alien turned to Cal and to Laura. "This . . . is the

one . . . you call your . . . brother?" he asked.

"Yes."

"I owe you both . . . much."

"No problem," said Laura.

"They've been expecting you," said Cal. "I think you're going to have a great time."

And then Shontill did something that shocked Laura. He smiled.

"I shall see you . . . again. That . . . I know."

So saying, he spun and leapt through the portal.

"Maybe sooner than you think," said Cal.

Chapter Twenty-four

Laura fled her pinnace the moment it was docked in the *Starbow*, grabbing Cal's hand and pulling him along. Klaxons reverberated through the corridors, and the call to battle stations sounded. Laura and Cal sprinted to the nearest lift, trying to get to the bridge as quickly as possible.

They leaned against the walls of the lift, panting. Shortly, she turned to him. "I know you're not really my brother, Cal."

Cal was dumbstruck. "Huh?"

"My good pal Zarpfrin told me. We'll talk about it later."

"But you are my sister . . ."

She glared at him. "I said, we'll talk about it when we have more time." She kissed him on the cheek. "But you know . . . It doesn't make any difference . . ."

Captain Northern met them on the bridge.

"How is Chivon Lasster?" was the first thing Laura wanted to know.

"She'll be okay. She's in sick bay now. Arkm's looking after her." He turned to Cal. "So, you're the infamous Cal Shemzak," he said. "The real Cal Shemzak . . ."

"Like I said, we had a little problem with a couple of those clones of yours," Laura explained.

"It's me!" said Cal. "And Captain, I just want to say that I truly appreciate all your help."

"Right now I think we'd better concentrate on getting out of here," said Northern. "It seems that we've run into some complications."

"Complications?"

"Yes. Mish didn't bother to tell us that we'd have to wait at least four hours to generate enough power to re-enter Underspace from the surface of a planet."

Mish's voice piped up. "I was never asked, Captain!" The doctor strolled over, looking terribly unconcerned. "Besides, I had no way of foreseeing the arrival of a fleet of Federation ships."

"Which are almost on top of us!" said Dansen Jitt. "We've got about a half hour at most before we'll be within range of their guns."

"Wonderful," said Laura. "So we've come all this way only to get finally blasted away by the Federation!"

"We can always surrender," said Cal.

"You don't know what we've done to Zarpfrin," said Laura. "His orders are probably to shoot first and ask for surrender later."

"Laura's right," said Captain Northern. "But there has to be another way."

"How long can our force screens hold out?" asked Cal.

"Not long."

"You have not asked for my thoughts on the matter," said Dr. Mish.

"You have an idea?"

"I was the one who suggested the mode of rescue that leaves us in this situation. It would seem likely, would it not, that I entertained various possibilities for modes of escape."

"We're all ears, Mish!" Laura exclaimed.

"Master Calspar . . . a question. I detect by certain sensory methods that you are still capable of mental contact with the array of your clones gathered in the Jaxdron enclosure."

Cal looked puzzled. "Really?"

"Give it a try."

Cal shrugged and closed his eyes, concentrating.

His eyes shot open.

"Yes!"

"In what state are they now?"

"Normal."

"And can you tell what the Jaxdron are doing?"

"They're apparently working on some different kind of escape. A particular starship is being repaired."

"Excellent. They are occupied, then, and will not interfere."

"Interfere with what?" demanded Northern.

"You will understand soon enough, Captain." He turned back to Cal. "I trust that since you have access to the clone matrix, you can still open the portal to Omega Space."

"Yes, of course. But what good will that do us in escaping from a fleet of Federation ships?" Cal asked, plainly mystified.

"You forget that I have certain mental powers of my own. Perhaps enough to step up your own abilities."

Laura understood. "You mean you're gonna make that portal large enough to fly the whole *Starbow* through?"

"That was my intention, yes," said Mish.

"It would be nice to consult with me. I *am* the captain!" said Northern.

Silver Zenyo called from the control board. "Captain! Federation ships approaching striking distance. Sensors indicate immediate deployment of nuclear missiles!"

"Get that damned hole open, Shemzak!" Northern ordered without batting an eye.

Cal sat down in a chair, shaking his head. "Any special way of doing this, Dr. Mish?"

"Just as before. Only do not limit the diameter of the portal."

"Right." Cal closed his eyes and began to concentrate.

"Now, Captain, if you would be so kind as to prepare the *Starbow* for a quick lateral movement via antigrav beams and rockets . . . . "

"Right away!" Northern stepped over and began issuing the necessary orders.

"Anything I can do?" Laura wanted to know.

"Perhaps strap yourself in. This might be a bumpy ride," returned Mish.

Laura obeyed, choosing a perch from which she could hear and observe all the proceedings.

She was most concerned about Cal, also seated. Mish had strapped Cal in, and he sat tensely, his face working with unreadable emotions as he concentrated on the problem.

Mish had taken a place nearby. He clearly had lost all awareness of the construct, focusing entirely upon a central source of thought.

Laura felt helpless; she wanted to help in some way, but knew there was nothing she could do.

She turned her attention to the vu-screens depicting the Jaxdron compound. Nothing moved. No sign of change.

In just a few seconds bridge activity lessened. The crew awaited words of command from the captain. But plainly the captain had no words to issue at the moment; he sat in his chair, awaiting an opportunity to command.

"Captain," said Tether Mayz at the communications terminal. "I'm getting a message from the Federation fleet. They've located us."

"Not surprising. Put it on the speakers, Tether. Let's see what they have to say."

A few deft movements on Mayz's part brought a voice with a recognizable Federation accent through the speakers.

" . . . here. Calling the Starship *Starbow*. Over."

"Let me speak to them," said Northern. "Put through our identity code."

"I think they know who we are by now," said Laura.

"Do it anyway."

There were some moments of silence, giving way to the same voice. "*Starbow*. We have you located. All modes of escape have been covered. This is Captain Neil Urnsur of the Federation Star Fleet. Our orders from Overfriend Zarpfrin are to destroy your ship upon sight. However, if you surrender immediately, I shall ignore those orders. I am not a bloodthirsty man, and I have indications that all is not right back on home base. However, should you refuse, I shall be forced to attack and destroy you. We have the necessary firepower to do so many times over, believe me, Captain!"

"How's it going, Cal?" Northern stage-whispered to Cal.

"It's working, sir," said Cal between clenched teeth. "I think it's working!"

"Good." The Captain switched on his radio extension and spoke. "Captain Urnsur! Frankly, we did not expect you to arrive so soon."

"Our forces have known for a long time about your destination, Captain. We only awaited orders. Now, will you surrender, or are you going to force us to destroy you?"

Suddenly, a message filled with static interrupted the conversation.

"Notice!" said a strangely accented voice. "This is a Jaxdron base, off-limits to Federation destructive activity by arrangement with Overfriend Zarpfrin. Do not fire upon this base!"

A time of silence as the captain of the Federation fleet no doubt mused on the situation.

"A Jaxdron base?" he said finally. "Our enemies . . . There is no order from Overfriend Zarpfrin concerning the sanctity of a Jaxdron base . . ."

"But this is not in the Game plan!" the voice fairly shrieked. "This is not in the arrangements. Our trust has been woefully abused! You will rue this, you and your Federation!"

"My orders, Captain Northern, are to deal with you. I no longer have any time to wait. What is your response?"

Laura was watching the vu-screens, and immediately noticed when something began happening on the Jaxdron base.

Something with round, sparkling edges was growing from the top.

The portal!

It was working!

Northern did not miss it. "That's it, I assume, Laura."

"Yes. That's it . . . only much bigger."

"Good." He flipped his switch. "Captain Urnsur, my response is *this*."

He executed a fruity Bronx cheer and immediately ordered a couple of *Starbow* missiles to be launched at the flagship.

"No!" came the strangled cry of the Jaxdron communicator before Northern ordered all radio contact shut down.

Northern smiled grimly. "Prepare for immediate departure from this universe, people!"

Laura saw that the aperture was still growing, looking now like some electric rainbow spanning the sky. And through it, a never-ending field swung away into what appeared to be a glorious dawn . . .

"Captain, the portal has just passed the dimensions necessary to pass through," reported Silver Zenyo.

"We've also got some nasty-looking missiles heading our way, Captain," said Dansen Jitt.

"Do we have those energy spokes of ours retracted as much as possible? I don't want to break any off!" said Northern. "Mish would be so pissed!"

"Yes sir, yes sir!" cried Dansen Jitt impatiently. "Let's get out of here!"

"Right! Full ahead, Silver. Gently, though!"

"Aye aye."

With unbearable slowness, the *Starbow* slipped along toward the portal. Its nose passed through, and the ship vibrated slightly.

"How's it holding up, Cal?" Northern asked.

"Fine, sir, but if you could speed it up . . . I can't promise how long I can keep it open."

"We're clear, Captain, on all sides," someone said.

"Maximum force, then."

The *Starbow* shot throught the portal into Omega Space.

"We're through, Captain."

"Yes. Cal, you may let the portal close."

Cal was sweating. "Yes, sir."

The vu-screens showed the portal rapidly growing smaller and smaller.

Just as it was about the size of a basketball, a flare of fire snaked through. And then the portal sealed entirely.

"We're safe!" Laura Shemzak whooped. "Safe!"

"Looks like the Jaxdron bit off more than they could chew," Cal said happily as he rose from his sitting position."

"The main force is not going to be very happy with Zarpfrin, that's for sure," Laura said. "Well, Cal. You know this new place we're in now. What's next?"

Cal Shemzak wiped his forehead and looked intently at Laura. "Well, I guess we'd better get on the good side of the natives here . . . the Frin'ral, that is . . ."

"Shontill should have put in a good word for us by now," said Northern.

"And then," Cal continued gravely.

The others listened intently.

"And then," he finished, smiling, "I'd like to go see a movie!"

Epilogue

The *Starbow* had landed.

It sat on the eternal plane called Omega Space, its engines idle, its energy screens off. No destination beckoned. No enemy threatened.

Nearby the spiraled towers and catwalks and twisted buildings of the Frin'ral city had materialized in curious harmony to the odd shape of the *Starbow*.

Between the two, on a grassy veranda, a party was taking place. A most unusual party.

"You see, it's all simply a matter of knowing how to adjust to the reality you find yourself in," said Cal Shemzak as he manufactured brightly colored balloons from the palms of his hands and sent them flying.

"You mean, like how you claim to be my brother?" Laura said briskly but playfully.

"Laura, I *am* your brother. You're saying you believe that rascal Zarpfrin over my word?" Cal feigned a look of hurt.

"I don't know who's more of a rascal, Cal," she said. She believed him, all right, she thought. She just wanted to let him dangle a while longer before she let him off the hook.

"So what were you saying, Calspar?" asked Chivon Lasster, looking much improved for being out in the fresh air.

"I don't think I even want to try it," said Arkm Thur, shaking his head.

"I don't like it here at all!" said Dansen Jitt. "It all gives me the willies!"

"Yeah," said Laura, reclining with a drink in her

hand. "And I suppose you'd rather be back in normal space being chased by the Federation!"

Jitt sat down. "Perhaps you're right. But how long do we have to stay here, anyway?"

Arkm Thur shrugged. "Who cares? Just consider it an extended vacation."

"I suppose we'll have to venture back soon enough to save the galaxy," Gemma Naquist said. "After all, Zarpfrin's still running about, and the Federation's still there . . . and just maybe there's a *real* war going on with the Jaxdron."

"Oh, will the macrocosmic conflict never cease?" said Cal softly, forming beautiful butterflies and sending them flying off into the breeze.

Laura sipped her drink and smiled over at him. She felt good. It was good to be back with Cal. And, being an eccentric himself, he fit in very well with this group.

They'd been in this strange dimension for two days now. At least, they knew them to be days because that was the way the *Starbow*'s clocks measured them. Shontill had indeed been of help in creating a peaceful coexistence with the Frin'ral. Even now, he and Dr. Mish were working with that civilization, learning much about the potential of this dimension, about the very fabric of the universe.

But some of the deeper mysteries of the *Starbow* apparently still eluded Mish, foremost among them the riddle of the origin of the starship and portal itself. If they had learned one thing for sure, it was that the strange device at the core of the *Starbow* had nothing to do with Omega Space. Working, it would apparently take them someplace else entirely . . .

No, this was most certainly only a brief layover, Laura knew. There were things to be accomplished out there in Normal Space. And perhaps beyond Normal Space as well, for Omega Space seemed something of a dimensional *cul de sac*. The adventures had not ceased, and the fight was not yet fully fought. No, far from it.

As for her, she knew that she could no longer experience life as she had before: as one long, erratic high. Her drug had kept her shielded from all but the more intense emotions. She had to experience everything now . . . even boredom. She would take it one day at a time. That, after all, was the way it came to her.

No, that wasn't quite true, she thought, savoring the delightfully tart punch that Cal had concocted. She did look forward to one thing. There was a spot of darkness deep inside her that she savored and nurtured secretly. Unhealthy? Perhaps. But it kept alive a spark of righteous indignation and desire for vengeance that might possibly help the *Starbow* in the future; it would certainly be a boon to the Free Worlds. And it would give her a dark and delightful joy when what she thought of was accomplished.

She was going to get Overfriend Arnal Zarpfrin.

All by herself.

And he was going to know that it was she on the triggering end of Death.

She smiled to herself as she listened to the wistful banter of the crew, lounging about fecklessly. The party was drifting peacefully along on the dregs of all the nervous energy that had been built up. Silver Zenyo suggested to Cal that a swimming pool might be nice, and Cal conjured one up. Silver shot off to get her bathing suit.

"How about you, Laura? You want to take a dip?" Cal asked.

"Are you kidding? With all the stuff in me, I would sink right to the bottom!"

"I could fix you up with some waterwings."

"No, thanks."

The flaps of nearby exotic tents rippled in the breeze. The smell of the recent barbecue they had enjoyed still flavored the air. The air was clear and invigorating, a climate that was a gentle balm to the soul. There was only one ingredient missing, and the lack of it irked Laura. "I wonder where Northern is?"

"Last time I saw him, he was still talking to Mish and the Frin'ral delegation . . . but then they seemed about finished and while Mish went off with Shontill and the others, Northern wandered back to the ship."

"He should be out here, with us," Laura said.

'Well, if he doesn't *want* to . . . " said Arkm Thur.

"It's his duty."

"So are you going to drag him out here?" asked Gemma Naquist playfully.

"No. I've got a better idea." She turned to her brother. "Cal, do you think that if we put our heads together on this one we can drag dear Captain Tars Northern out here with the rest of his crew?"

Cal nodded casually. "Sure, as long as he doesn't oppose it."

"I don't see how he could."

"Okay," said Cal. "Just remember how I told you to do it."

Laura nodded, and then closed her eyes, visualizing Captain Tars Northern, wanting him there, imagining him there.

Tars Northern, she mused idly. Something else she was going to have to take one step at a time.

She opened eyes, and he was there.

"Good show," someone cried.

Northern looked disheveled and bemused. In one hand was a brandy bottle, and in the other was a half-empty glass.

"I'm pretty drunk," he said. "Must be. Don't remember coming here. Just as well though. Meant to. Just got carried away."

"Celebrating, Northern?" asked Cal.

Northern shook his head. "Nope. Just doing this one last time. Mish is taking me off the stuff. For a long time, he says. Just as well, I suppose. No matter what the remedy, it's really no good for you." He took a swig.

"Join the club, Northern," said Laura, hoisting a bottle of punch.

"I think I started the damned club," said Northern.

"So, did everything go well with the Frin'ral?" asked Gemma.

"Oh, yeah. Sure. Only one problem."

"What's that?"

"We have a problem getting out! With Cal Shemzak's clone matrix destroyed, it's taking us a while to figure out how to open a hole big enough to get the *Starbow* through!"

The crew seemed nonplussed.

"What?" Laura said first, speaking for them all.

"Oh, I shouldn't worry," said Cal. "We'll work something out." His expression grew slightly more doubtful as he thought about it. "I hope."

"Yeah. I hope so, too," said Northern. "And there are a lot of things to be settled back where we come from."

"And light-years to go before we sleep, eh Captain?" said Cal.

"That's right." The Captain finished the brandy in the glass and poured another. "Long as Mish ain't here, might as well drink up!"

"You know, Mr. Jitt," said Cal. "Laura was telling me about that vision you had. Sounds as though it was accurate, but in strange ways."

Jitt shook his head. "Well, if the captain is swearing off strong drink, I'm swearing off strong visions. No more for me! I'm just going to be a plain old navigator!"

"Yeah. I can see how that final battle was reasonably accurate," said Laura. "But that business you mentioned about Captain Northern lying on the ground and me laughing. It's ludicrous!"

Jitt shrugged. "Sorry. I don't know where it came from."

"Captain," said Laura. "Where do you think that kind of thing comes from? You think the Frin'ral might be able to give us an inkling . . . Captain? Captain!"

Northern did not respond. He lay still in his chair, clutching his bottle.

"Captain!" said Laura, getting up and going to him. She shook his shoulder.

Northern slipped from the chair onto the ground.

The starship captain began to snore.

"Well," said Cal Shemzak. "Jitt was right after all. Northern's dead all right. Dead *drunk!*"

And Laura Shemzak began to laugh.

1-800-223-0510

Berkley Publishing Group

200 Madison Ave

New York NY
10016

1-800-631-8571 ext 445

SPECIAL ORDER PAPERBACK CARD
(Please Print)

NAME: James Bakeman

ADDRESS: POB x 201

Rockville 56369

PHONE: [Home] 252-3222

[Business]

Title: Galactic Warriors

Author: Bischoff

Quantity:

Hardcover Price:

Paperback Price: 2 95

SKU: 5134671

Publisher: Berkley

Jobber: 0441 2 72589 1

Stock Number

Date Requested: 8/15